Rachael Stewart adores ⬚⬚⬚
heartwarmingly romantic ⬚⬚⬚
writing since she could p⬚⬚
of scrawled-on pages in h⬚⬚
at heart, she now lives in Yorkshire, with her very own
hero and three awesome kids—and if she's not tapping
out a story she's wrapped up in one or enjoying the great
outdoors. Reach her on Facebook, Twitter (@rach_b52) or at
rachaelstewartauthor.com.

J. Margot Critch currently lives in St John's,
Newfoundland, with her husband Brian and their two little
buddies, Simon and Chibs. She spends equal amounts of
time writing, listening to Jimmy Buffett's music and looking
out at the ocean—all the while trying to decide if she wants
coffee or a margarita.

**If you liked *Naughty or Nice* and
A Sinful Little Christmas
why not try**

The Deal by Clare Connelly
Turn Me On by Dylan Rose

Discover more at millsandboon.co.uk

NAUGHTY OR NICE

RACHAEL STEWART

A SINFUL LITTLE CHRISTMAS

J. MARGOT CRITCH

MILLS & BOON

First Published in Great Britain 2019
by Mills & Boon, an imprint of HarperCollins*Publishers*
1 London Bridge Street, London, SE1 9GF

Naughty or Nice © 2019 Rachael Stewart

A Sinful Little Christmas © 2019 J. Margot Critch

ISBN-13: 978-0-263-27394-6

MIX
Paper from
responsible sources
FSC™ C007454

This book is produced from independently certified FSC™ paper
to ensure responsible forest management.
For more information visit www.harpercollins.co.uk/green.

Printed and bound in Spain
by CPI, Barcelona

NAUGHTY OR NICE

RACHAEL STEWART

MILLS & BOON

To my kids, who will be doing their utmost to get on Santa's nice list!

I know you're too young to read this—in fact, you'll always be too young—but I can't have a Christmas book without dedicating it to you.

I love you regardless of your naughty little antics.

To my family and friends for making every Christmas as special as it can be.

And to my gorgeous readers, too… Are you on the naughty or nice list this year?

How about joining me and straddling them both?
Ho ho ho ;-)

Happy Christmas to all, and to all a good read!

R xx

PROLOGUE

I TWIST MY hands in front of me, the heel of one stiletto grinding into the plush carpet of my father's study.

I know Lucas is going to follow me here. I saw it in his eyes. That same look I've caught several times over in the past few months…the same look I know I sport: want, desire—*love*.

I've loved him for years—long before Mum and Dad became his guardians…long before I really knew what it was that had my heart trying to leap out of my chest, my body throbbing, my tongue tied.

I'm eighteen. It's my birthday party. It's as good a time as any to tell him—or so I keep telling myself. I can't go on keeping it locked up inside. But I'm scared. It doesn't matter that I sense he feels the same, that I see the way he looks at me when he thinks no one else is watching.

I pin his expression in my mind, focus on it as I grab my flute of champagne and throw back the remainder. The hit of alcohol makes me wince, but I need it—Dutch courage. I return it to the side as I watch the door.

You love him. You can tell him. You have to.

I hear footsteps in the hallway, louder than the music from my party, underway further down the hall, and I take a breath, pressing my hands into my thighs, forcing them to still and hoping their dampness doesn't mark the bright white of my dress.

The door opens and I can't breathe.

'Evangeline?'

His voice sends blood rushing through my body, my pulse rate skittering out of control.

'Yes…' It comes out like a whisper, my fear coming through, and it frustrates me. I want to be confident. I want him to see me as a woman, not the little sister of his best friend, Nate.

Get it together.

His head appears around the door, his gaze hesitant as he looks from me to the hallway and back again.

'Hey.'

He steps inside but pauses, the confident twenty-one-year-old I usually see oddly absent. He's boyish, uncertain, and my heart turns over.

'Hey,' I manage back, breathless.

We don't move closer. My knees feel like jelly and his fingers tremble a little as he rakes one hand through his hair, his other still hanging on to the door handle.

Take control. You need to do this. You need to show him.

'Close the door.'

I'm surprised at the confidence I've injected into my tone—am surprised all the more when he does what I ask. But his eyes don't return to me. They burn a hole in the floor at his feet.

I take a small breath. 'Why won't you look at me?'

His eyes waver and I can sense the fight in him.

I step forward, my progress slow as the tight mini-dress restricts my movement, riding ever higher up my thighs. The moment I'd chosen it I'd had this in mind. To confess my love, maybe even seduce him. I want my first time to be with him and tonight would be so perfect.

'Lucas?'

He shakes his head, but then his eyes lock with mine and I feel their burn. Need is etched in the tightness of his jaw, in his hands fisting at his sides.

'We shouldn't be in here...alone.'

'Then why did you come?' I press.

Please let him be torn. Please let him confirm what I suspect.

'I—'

He shakes his head again but his eyes are still fixed on mine. His internal fight is clear in their depths, and he runs his teeth over his lower lip. The move distracting me with the glimpse of his tongue, the mouth I so desperately want to taste.

'Being alone with you, like this...' He waves a hand up and down my length, his eyes travelling over me and setting my skin alight.

'Don't trust yourself?' I tease, forcing out the playful jest even though I know how much rides on his response.

I pause less than an arm's reach away and look up at him from beneath my lashes, not quite ready to reach for him. That fear of rejection is still there.

'You know we shouldn't.'

It's my turn to shake my head. 'Why?'

'Because—because of who you are. Of who your family are to me.'

'In a way, we're your family too.'

'Exactly, Eva—they're all I have.'

I risk another step and hold his tormented gaze. I want to kiss it away, take away the pain of his past, his loss, his loneliness. He never had a father. His mother, although best friend to my own, was hardly ever present, and now she's been dead almost a year. But I have been here. I've always been here for him. I can be enough. If only he will see it.

'And we will always be here for you. But I have to tell you how I feel. I have to tell you I…I…' My voice cracks and I curse the show of weakness.

'Don't, Evangeline—don't say it.'

His words are a warning that I can't abide, and it's the push that I need.

'Why?'

'Because it will change everything.'

'And why is that so bad?'

He takes a breath and it shudders out of him, but he says nothing.

Now. It has to be now.

'Lucas.' I slip my hands over his shoulders, feel him tense beneath them, but there's no going back. 'I love you.'

He squeezes his eyes shut, closing me out, and when he opens them again they're blazing. His hands are reaching out, tight on my hips as he forces me away.

'I love you too, but not—not like *this*. I can't.'

He turns to leave and I move, stepping between him and his escape, so swift that he ends up pressed against me, my back against the door as my lips part on a gasp.

It's not just surprise—it's the strange frisson that runs right down my front as my body absorbs his heat, the very hardness of him.

His eyes drop to my mouth and there's no need for words. His intent sears me seconds before his lips claim mine.

Christ, I'm in heaven.

He isn't soft, tentative, uncertain. He's hard, determined, his tongue forcing my mouth apart, demanding entry, coaxing me into doing the same.

I've been kissed before, and I've kissed boys before, but I've never been devoured—not like this.

My body thrums, my breasts prickle against his chest, and the dull ache in my gut swells and throbs with mindless need. My hands are in his hair, clinging him to me, his own rake over my body, feverish, trembling. I can't believe this is real. I feel drugged, dreaming.

And then he groans into my mouth, pressing me back harder, and I know it's real. I know this is happening… my dream is coming true.

His fingers drop to my naked thighs, encouraging my dress higher. I don't know whether I lift my leg to hook it around him or he does, but the hard swell of him inside his jeans presses at the throbbing heart of me and I moan my pleasure.

He curses, his teeth nipping at my lip as he shakes his head once more. 'I've wanted you, so long.'

His confession jerks me alert. I want more of it. More words. More to affirm how he feels.

'How long?'

'Too long.'

Happiness bursts within me. Everything's falling into place.

I find his lips again, desperate to seal his words with my kiss. 'And you can have me. I'm yours. I've always been yours.'

There's a strange knocking sound—one that doesn't compute with the whirlwind that is my mind—and suddenly I'm thrust away from him. I try to focus through the haze. I see his widened gaze, his alarm clear.

'Lucas? You in there?'

The handle shifts with my brother's voice, but the door doesn't budge. I realise Lucas has turned the latch. It fills me with hope, but hope dies just as swiftly. He looks as if he's seen a ghost as he stares at me in horror.

'Lucas! Come on, man. Someone said they saw you head in here... Eva too.'

Oh, God.

He was pale before. Now he looks deathly. His eyes leave me, his head shaking.

'I'm an idiot. A *fucking* idiot.'

He says it under his breath and I tiptoe towards him, my hand reaching out. But he moves away from me just as quickly, his eyes throwing daggers. 'Don't.'

There are footsteps down the corridor and then my father's voice. 'What's going on?'

'Nothing… I'm just getting Eva. Mum wants her to cut the cake.'

'The last place Eva will be is in my study, son.'

Nate gives an awkward laugh. 'Sure…of course. I'll check upstairs.'

They move off, their voices growing distant, and I know my brother is protecting us. But I don't want protection. I don't want to hide any more.

'Lucas, please don't push me away. I don't want to deny this any more. I know you feel the same. I know you—'

'You don't know anything.'

'You want me—'

'Yes, I want you.' He launches the words at me, so certain. 'But that's not love.'

'It is—because I love you.'

'You don't love me. You're infatuated, confused, doped up on hormones.'

My heart starts to split in two, ice running through the middle. 'You don't know what you're talking about…'

'I know you and your family are all that I have. That without you I have nothing.'

I don't know what to say to that. I know the truth of it. But it makes my reasoning all the more valid. It's so simple.

'Then accept that we love one another and that my family will be happy for us. Once they adjust.'

His head shakes violently. 'No, they won't. Don't you see? Nate was banging this door down to *stop* us. He *knows*.'

'But—'

'No, Eva, he's already made it clear you're off-limits and, hell, he's right. What happens to me a year or two down the line when this…whatever this is…fizzles out?'

'It won't.'

'You can guarantee that, can you?'

'I…I…'

He rakes both hands through his hair, his torment written in his haunted brown eyes. Eyes I've dreamed about for so long.

And then he's turning away and heading for the door.

'Please,' I hear myself say. 'Don't go.'

He doesn't even pause—doesn't even look back as he unlocks the door and slips away. Leaving me standing there, my heart in tatters, as I realise he means it.

That no matter how much I love him he can never be mine.

CHAPTER ONE

THIS IS MY MOMENT. For the first time in my life I know that I've made it. That I stand apart. My family name hasn't handed me this. Aside from a small investment from dear old Ma and Pa, this is all me.

My baby is finally ready, and companies are clambering over themselves to head up its manufacture, its distribution, wanting to join forces, to conquer the field.

But I have weeks to decide.

Tonight is about enjoying the buzz…feeding it.

The room is fit to bursting with prospective producers and vendors alike. And here's me, confident in a festive red silk dress that just sweeps the floor, my blonde hair knotted up high, sophisticated, yet softened by the loose locks that fall free. The delicate bubbles of the champagne in my hand are feeding my ego and my mood to perfection.

'Well, you did it, angel.'

I turn and lift my chin to meet my father's eye. I can see the admiration in his gaze—something I've hungered for since I found I could outrun my brother at fourteen.

It's not that I'm naturally competitive, but when you're always deemed the less capable, the *girl*, it can happen. Even more so when your brother can apparently do no wrong, when in truth he does plenty wrong, and *still* has admiration dished out in spades.

'I know.'

He tenses, and I fear he's read the bitterness in my tone. But, no, his eyes leave me and narrow. Something else has caught his attention.

'What the hell...?' he mutters.

I follow his line of sight, but already my nerves sizzle. My father doesn't ever show unease—he doesn't do emotion, particularly in a business setting like tonight's launch party. *My* launch party.

'Did you invite him?'

'Wh—?' The word dies and my entire body draws tight.

I see him. I see the exact cause of my father's unease and feel it seep into my very skin. My mood dies with it. The champagne flute trembles in my hand and I know I should look away, but I can't.

Ten years and still my eyes are hooked on him.

Lucas Waring.

My family's nemesis.

My heart's downfall.

'No,' I manage to say.

I shouldn't be surprised—not when the room is full of his peers.

Peers? Are you dreaming?

They're not his equal. No one is. Waring Holdings has it all and now here is Lucas, wanting...*what?*

'He can't possibly think you'll be interested in working with him.'

My father speaks my mind exactly. He can't. But what else?

'There's only one way to find out.'

I'm not the eighteen-year-old girl I once was, and I'm not the woman I became soon after that, determined to evade him. I am in control now. This is my night. This is work.

'Excuse me.'

'No.' My father steps into my path. 'I'll get rid of him.'

I hold his eye as my lips twitch. What I want to say is *Stop treating me like a child*, but in my mind that sounds petulant and childlike in itself. Instead I smile up at him. 'He's made the effort to come. I should at least see what he wants.'

'But—'

'But nothing, Dad. Giving someone as powerful as Lucas the cold shoulder tonight of all nights would send the wrong message to the room.'

My father grunts and swigs his champagne. He knows I'm right. He didn't get where he is today by letting personal differences get in his way. But then it's the first time I'm aware of that Lucas has dared venture near any of us in five long years.

Ever since my family shut him out and the blame

for the demise of the company he co-owned with Nate seemed to land firmly at his feet.

I questioned it at the time. I continued to question it each and every time Nate screwed up after that. It couldn't have been down to Lucas—not entirely. But it seems Lucas has suffered the same as me.

Nate's golden halo failed to shift.

I can't deny I'm curious as to what truly went down. And I also can't deny that his presence here tonight only serves to help my cause, my product. It'll feed the frenzy already taking hold as companies vie for my business.

Or it'll send them running, because they'll think there's no chance in hell you'll look anywhere else but him.

Not him—his business, Eva!

I give my head a small shake, the loose curls from my updo brushing against the prickled skin of my nape. It loosens up my thoughts, the tension.

'Why don't you make sure Mum doesn't flip at his presence?' I say, and with another sip of champagne I start to make my way towards him, praying he doesn't spy me before I'm prepared.

But already his head is turning, as if he senses my approach, and then his eyes are locked on mine and I can feel a startling rush through my system. It doesn't matter that I'm used to the sight of him on the TV, in the tabloids—that same old zing is in my belly, that heat that only his physical presence has ever instilled creeping into my cheeks.

I want to look away, but I won't give him that. I am stronger now, wiser, and the better for it. And so I enjoy him, my eyes sweeping over every inch of him. His black hair, long on top. His prominent brow arching over heavy-lashed eyes that narrow on me, dark and intense. I ignore the hiccup to my pulse and cut lower, to his wide, angular jaw with its intentional stubble.

I avoid his mouth entirely.

I don't need the memory of its brief contact all those years ago. *I really don't.*

I move my eyes lower, to the broad set of his shoulders—wider than I recall. Imposing. I don't dwell on the muscle behind that. Instead I focus on the designer cut of his deep grey suit, the white shirt and his defiantly skinny black tie.

My lips lift at the edges, I can't help it. *Always the rebel...*

I lift my eyes back to his and they flicker. There's something there. I just don't know what. Unease?

Maybe.

Like hell.

He owns the room. His presence commands attention even when he's not looking for it. Just like he's commanding my own, against my will.

A waiter passes between us and he reaches out for a glass, but not once does his gaze release me, and I can feel myself being drawn in like the besotted eighteen-year-old I once was.

Careful, Eva.

'Lucas…'

I draw his name out, feel it fall softly from my lips, and I see his eyes flit to them. I know they're red and glossy. The perfect match for my dress and the countrywide festivities, and I imagine him looking hungrily over them now.

If only…

'I wish I could say it's a pleasure to see you.'

I'm proud of the steadiness in my voice, its hard edge—it's what he deserves for what he did to me ten years ago and for the last five, too, if my family are right… In this second I'm not sure which I want to hurt him more for.

Yes, you do…liar.

He watches me with that intense stare that I can't even begin to read and raises his glass to his lips. Too late I'm looking, remembering, and my betraying tongue sweeps over my own lips…

'It's rude to stare.'

My eyes leap and I curse his very presence, his very effect over me. But there's a tightness to his voice, a flare to his eyes that he cannot hide, and I know he's not immune to me—not any more. It gives me power and I feed on it.

'It's rude to attend a party without an invitation.'

He smiles, the movement small and soft—and, *dammit*, my insides quiver.

'I'm used to being welcomed with open arms. Invited or not.'

I raise my brow, the idea of being close enough to embrace him not helping my focus.

It's a figure of speech, idiot.

I cock my head, masking my unease. 'Once upon a time that may have been true, but not here, not now, and not with me.'

'Not with you, or not with your family, Evangeline?'

If I could melt to the floor I would. No one calls me Evangeline—no one. Unless they're my parents. I am Eva—strong, dependable, Eva. A woman who has proved her worth a hundred times over.

But when *he* says it, the *way* he says it, it's not like Mum and Dad do it. It doesn't make me feel like a girl, weak and vulnerable. I feel empowered, worthy of so much, catapulted onto a pedestal and ready to be worshipped.

By him. At my feet.

Oh, yes.

I swallow, the bolt through my body jolting me straight.

It scares me. *He* scares me. And I know I need him gone—that no matter what I said to Dad I don't dare to entertain him for longer than is necessary.

'Cat got your tongue?'

'No,' I blurt.

'So?'

I can see a pulse working in his jaw, and his eyes are intense as they watch and wait for my response.

'Is it you or your family telling me I'm not welcome, Evangeline?'

'Both.' I say it and immediately regret it. It's too per-

sonal, too unprofessional, but I can't think clearly. Not
with him so close.

'Is that your way of asking me to leave?'

I sense nearby heads turning, ears tuning in.

Careful, Eva...

I'm losing myself in the fierce glint of her blue gaze,
almost daring her to throw me out. There's something
about the fight in her that I want to provoke.

It's so much easier than dealing with all the shit buried ten years deep.

'No, Lucas, I'm not asking you to leave.'

She wets her lips. Again. And the red shines ever
deeper, the carnal colour driving a string of sinful
thoughts—none of which have a place in this room,
with this audience.

Or fit with the reason you're here.

It's about business.

Not her.

Not…

A pulse flutters in her throat and she raises her hand,
her red-tipped fingers circling over the delicate ripple.
Christ, I want to do that—be the person with his fingers over that creamy skin.

I tighten my hold on the stem of the glass, slipping
my other hand inside my pocket. Out of trouble.

'Good.' I tear my eyes away, looking towards the
grand Christmas tree and the big screen that stands
proud alongside it, streaming highlights of the product

I'm here to secure. 'Because I think we have a future together...in business.'

I suck the inside of my cheek.

In business? What the actual fuck? Do you want to make it any more obvious you want her in your bed too?

I hear her laugh, and the sound is as surprising as its effect, rippling through my body like an aftershock. I'd forgotten how she can do that—be it with a laugh, a smile or a song when she thinks no one's listening.

'Of course, Lucas. Of course in business. What else could you possibly be suggesting?'

She watches me over the rim of her glass, the depths of her eyes alive with suggestion, amusement, confidence. And it's the confidence that's my undoing. It's new. To me, at least. Where there was once a questioning innocence there's now the maturity of a woman who knows her own mind, her own desires.

And where do those desires lie now?

Ten years ago she made it obvious, but now...

Hell, most women desire me—it's par for the course. My money and power attract all sorts, even without the body I work hard to hone.

But you don't care about other women. You only care for her.

Cared—not *care*. Because that would be damn stupid.

Ten years ago she was forbidden. As the sister of my best friend, as the daughter of the closest thing I had to parents—*real* parents.

But, let's face it, here I am now, her family's worst nightmare, and all that loyalty no longer applies.

Just think what you can do with that.

I look her over, slowly, purposefully, and before I can hold back it's out. 'It wasn't my intention—I came here tonight to secure a deal, to offer you a very lucrative contract… But now I find myself wanting a whole lot more.'

Her eyes widen and the glass quivers beneath her chin, not quite lowering but not quite lifting either. She's shocked and I seize the advantage.

'What's it been, Evangeline—seven years?'

'Six.'

She says it so certainly it makes me wonder. Has she counted it down to the exact day, the exact moment? Because I sure as hell have, despite my intentional miscalculation. And even then it had been a brief passing—a moment at the Beaumonts' home before Nate and I flew out on business. But it's ingrained in my memory. The sight of her with another man—her *fiancé*. Happy.

'How is Peter?'

I don't know why I even ask it. I can see she isn't married—her bare finger gives that away. And there's no reason for me to think he's still on the scene, so why I need the added reassurance is beyond me.

'I have no idea. We broke up not long after that night.'

My question hasn't even jarred her, and that tells me enough. She remembers the occasion.

I don't want to feel the pleasure-filled rush that

comes from this, but it's there anyway—as is the burning need to taste those lips that keep goading me with their illicit colour, their inviting sheen.

'And Nate?' I manage to ask. 'I can't see him here.'

Her lashes flutter at my change in focus. Moving from one unsettling topic to another. But the need to talk business, to get back to safer ground, is lost on me.

'My brother had some work to tie up in Hong Kong. He'll be back for Christmas.'

I nod and ignore the weird ache her mention of Christmas kick-starts inside me. Christmas at the Beaumonts' was my tradition for so long. I never dwell on how much I miss it, but in that second I feel it. The cold, dull ache of what once existed but is no more.

And Nate still has it all, whereas I—

For fuck's sake, Lucas, get with it!

'Good for him.' I crush the ache, but the bitterness is there in the chill of my tone.

Her eyes narrow and I look away, forcing my shoulders to relax as I sip at my drink, wanting to quash the past just as much as I want it brought to the fore and dealt with.

But what would that accomplish? *Nothing.*

'I see your parents made it.' I gesture to where they're standing together at the bar, their eyes drawn to us as inconspicuously as they can manage. But I know they are watching. I can feel their penetrative stare as much as I can feel the heat of her proximity.

'They wouldn't miss it. It's in their interest to see me and my business do well.'

'I understand they have a twenty-five per cent share?'

'You've done your research.'

'I *always* do my research.'

I trust no one. Not any more. What little trust I ever gave was destroyed by her brother five years ago.

'I make it my business to know all there is about the companies I wish to work with *and* the people who run them.'

'And what does your research tell you about me?'

'You or your business?'

'Both.'

If it had been any other woman I might have thought she was fishing, but looking into her eyes I see she is not. That fierceness is still there, that sense that she has proved herself over and over again, and knows I won't have found her wanting. And it drives me to the brink.

Would that confidence extend to the bedroom too?

'Your product has an eager market, but its patent will only protect it for so long. Time is of the essence, and you need a ready production line and a route to market that is as speedy as we can make it.'

'We?' Her brows rise. 'That's quite presumptuous of you.'

'You know my company can give you both.'

She hums low in her throat and it resonates through me. My eyes fall to her lips, to their provocatively tight line. How I want to probe it with my tongue…make her yield…

'And what of me, Lucas? What does your research tell you about me?'

I want to tell her that I'd value her business, but more than that, I'd value *her*. I want to tell her that I'd trust her. That everything I knew of her all those years ago hasn't really changed…that all I've learned in the intervening years only reinforces that view. That there is nothing in her to spark my doubt.

Except my experience with her brother—an experience which has made me an outcast of her family…

You're getting personal. This is business. You only have to trust her as far as the contract you draw up dictates.

Yet already I can feel myself wanting more. Wanting to see how far I can push the perfect, composed businesswoman before me and make her crack. Make her desire me like her eighteen-year-old self did.

If only I could go back, take what she offered so willingly instead of—

'Are you ready, Eva? The floor awaits you.'

It's her father. He appears by her side from out of nowhere. Fuck her red lips. If not for those I would have sensed his approach. Been ready for it. Instead I'm forced to look straight from them to him, and I can see displeasure in every hard-cut line to his face.

It's as if he can see inside my soul to the ingrained need I have for his daughter and is telling me where to shove it.

'Mr Beaumont.' I say it smoothly and raise my glass, giving him the half-smile I reserve for business.

His eyes flash. I can see he wants to ignore me, and

Eva positively thrums with tension as her gaze flits between us.

'Yes, of course—thank you, Dad.'

She lifts a hand to her father's chest, clearly telling him to stand down, and it riles my blood. I'm not a man to tell tales, and I'm not about to start now, but the truth of what happened five years ago is burning to get out.

I wash it back with champagne and turn to Eva, my hand falling to the curve of her back as I move to speak and feel the words evaporate on the heat of her skin beneath the silk.

She turns to look at me, her mouth parting in what I think is surprise—until I see the flush to her cheeks, the flare to her eyes, and I know, in that moment, that she feels it too. The desire. And if I were a betting man I'd put money on it being stronger than ever before.

'Let's talk later.'

I don't wait for a response. I turn and walk away. Seeking out the shadows where I can regain my prized composure in peace.

I'm not used to losing my cool. I depend on it to face the many challenges that come my way. But something tells me that working with Evangeline would be a challenge like no other—because, regardless of my intentions when I set out tonight, I want her.

Her *and* her business.

Trouble is, I know which one I want more…

I watch as she takes to the podium, her entire body glinting under the fairy lights of the tree, and my body stiffens with a need so fierce I know it should have me running in the opposite direction and yet I'm rooted.

I owe the Beaumonts nothing.

But I owe *her* a ten-year-old debt. And suddenly I can't wait to pay up in full.

CHAPTER TWO

I DELIVER MY speech to the room and my words flow. I've rehearsed them a zillion times over and could do it in my sleep. Which is a good job, considering my attention is off the product and on the dark corner of the room where I know *he* waits. Listening...

I can feel his intense stare, his hunger. It was there in his touch, in his eyes that burned into my back all the way to the podium, and it's still there, fuelling my own.

The audience is enraptured. I've been reeling them in for the last twenty minutes. But still my mouth dries with anticipation. For *him*.

I pause to sip some champagne, my smile sweeping the entire audience before coming back to him. I need this to be sated. Before it consumes my every thought, drives my every action.

I raise my glass and offer a toast to the future. It's an excuse to loosen my vocal cords further, before I leave the stage and do what's expected of me—circulate the room.

Most people I've spoken to already. But now it's

about verbally agreeing to meetings and having my PA follow them up. Sealing their interest.

I know *he* will be on that list of interested parties. I owe it to my product.

It won't sit well with my family, but I'll deal with that as I do any business dealing—with professionalism. My parents can't fault me for that, and whatever deal I sign will buy them out. It's money back in their pocket and the business wholly my own. It's what I've dreamed of for so long. And if that money comes from a deal with Lucas, so be it.

Yeah, and what about Nate?

I bury the instinctive snort. I'm sick of him getting a free ride. I love him. I do. But I'm almost certain that whatever happened five years ago had more to do with him than the tale I've been given: that Lucas simply ran when the going got tough, leaving Nate and my father to clean up the mess.

But what about what he did to you? What about your heart?

Now my tummy turns over. My heart has no place in this. Not any more. I will consider his business offer, but as for the unvoiced part of his proposition…

I find him in the room. He leans against a pillar, one leg crossed over the other, his body relaxed. But his eyes as they lock with mine are anything but.

I moisten my lips. For that my body is already willing—my eighteen-year-old self still craving satisfaction, longing to experience what he cruelly refused all those ago. Only this time it'll be on *my* terms.

I'll show him what he's been missing, get this carnal need sated, and then it can all be about business.

If I choose to sign with him.

'You were amazing, Eva.'

I drag my eyes away to smile at Clare. She's a fabulous assistant—her excitement bubbles over as if it were my own. 'Thank you.'

'If anyone had the slightest doubt they'll be utterly convinced now that they want it—even if it's to gain a piece of *you*.'

I know she means it professionally, but I can't help thinking of Lucas, and again I'm distracted, my eyes hunting him out. And then a crazy urge takes over.

'Clare, do me a favour and hold the room for five. I just need to take care of something.'

'Sure.'

I'm already heading for the exit, the restrooms, giving a polite 'I'll be back in just a moment...' to anyone who pauses to speak to me.

I know I don't need to beckon him, that he'll be hot on my tail. And he is. As soon as my hand presses into the restroom door he's at my back.

'Escaping?'

I turn and smile up at him. 'Wait here.'

His brow pinches together. He's unaccustomed to being commanded—that's obvious. But he does as he's told and I walk through the door, scanning the stalls. They're all empty and I don't hang around. I pull open the door and reach for the skinny black tie that reminds me so much of the defiant teen I loved.

'Come.'

I walk backwards and he moves with me, feeding the power swimming like liquid heat through my veins, my core.

'What is this, Eva?'

'What do you think?'

'I hope it's you calling in a ten-year debt.'

I keep moving, ignoring the brief spike of pain, of heartbreak. Knowing I'm about to replace it with something far more satisfying.

'Do you remember that night?'

His jaw clenches, his eyes ablaze, and I know he's reliving it.

'Yes,' he grinds out.

His tension is palpable and I take conceited pleasure in it.

'I remember.'

I push open a stall door, thankful for the opulent finish, and nudge him inside. A toilet wouldn't be my ideal place to feed this need, but it's certainly the most convenient. And, as far as toilets go, this is designed for a certain clientele—a sleek private vanity area, with space for a woman's multitude of possessions or her derriere, should the need arise. How very convenient.

I back him inside, blindly locking the door behind me. 'Do you remember how you left me?'

He falters and shakes his head.

'No?' I raise my brow at him, my fingers toying with the slit in the silk that rides high up my thigh.

'I do remember.'

His voice is tight. It reverberates through my spine as I circle the exposed skin and raise the slit higher. '*What* do you remember, Lucas?'

'I remember you wore a white number that barely covered your arse.'

I can feel the effort it takes him to form the words and my confidence edges ever higher. I hook my fingers into the fabric of my dress and spread it open across my thigh, loving how his eyes track the move, his breath hitching.

'What else?'

'I remember how your skin felt beneath my palms… the taste of champagne on your tongue.'

He gives a small shudder and his fists flex at his sides. I know he wants to reach for me, but something is stopping him. And I'm glad. I want to be in control. The one driving this…

I lift the fabric until it exposes the lace of my nude thong and watch him swallow heavily.

'Do you want to know what *I* remember, Lucas?'

His eyes lift to mine, burning deep, and I don't wait for his answer. I focus on the sex, the need, the desire that has lived on in spite of my shattered heart.

'I remember aching for you so badly… I remember being wet and ready for you…'

I ease my hand between my parted legs and he exhales sharply, his eyes falling away once more, his fists tight.

'I can remember wanting to do just this…'

I slip my fingers beneath the lace. Christ, I'm so wet. My thong is damp against the backs of my fingers. *He* does this to me. Without a touch he has me primed and ready.

I catch my lower lip in my teeth as I pull my fingers back over my clit, pleasure ripping through me, my hips gyrating into their touch. His eyes flare and I lock onto them, getting off on his reaction as much as the skilful touch of my own fingers.

I could come like this. I know it. Come and leave. Make him suffer. But it's not enough.

'Come here,' I tell him.

He doesn't hesitate. He steps forward, his hands reaching to cup my face, but I lean away from him. I don't want him to kiss me. Not on my lips at any rate. It's too personal—too close to my teenage dreams.

I press my free hand to his chest and look up into his questioning gaze. 'Make me come.'

He cocks a grin at me. 'My pleasure.' He lowers his hand.

'No.'

He frowns.

'With your mouth.'

His eyes widen. 'You like being in charge now?'

'Always.'

I slip my hand out of my thong and gather up the skirt of my dress. 'On your knees.'

As he follows my instructions, surprise floods me. I didn't expect this swift agreement. And then he's upon me, his mouth encasing my mound through the lace, the heat of his breath making me shudder, and my knees go weak.

He probes me with his tongue, his teasing through the fabric enough to make my legs buckle completely. He palms my behind. Holding me steady.

'Why don't you sit?' he murmurs against me, encouraging me to the countertop. I go willingly, my dress hitched up to my hips, and the cold surface a shock to the cheeks of my arse. I spasm and he laughs. The sound resonates over my clit.

'Easy...'

I fork my hand over his head and draw him against me. My other hand clutches the edge of the countertop. 'I don't want easy.'

This time his laugh is tight, and his eyes are now black with his own need. He catches the lace of my thong in his teeth and tugs. 'These need to go'

I am captivated by him. For all I want to be in charge, I would actually let him do anything to me in this moment. I nod my head, my hand releasing him to grip the countertop.

He takes hold of the waistband just as the sound of people approaching reaches us—the unmistakable click of stilettos, women talking. The door opens and I tense. My eyes widen on to his, but he merely smiles as he continues with his task.

A stall door opens, a tap runs. The women are still talking, but I'm not listening. I'm focused entirely on not giving us away, my knuckles white with the effort of holding everything in as well as keeping my perch upon the vanity.

He shimmies down my thong, the thin cord stinging

against my skin as he pulls it from underneath me. He brings it to my calves but doesn't take it off. Instead he bends forward and lifts my ankles, ducking to position himself between my legs. The sharp points of my heels dig into his tailored jacket and for a split second I worry about damaging it—but then his eyes lock with mine and my brain empties.

I am spread open and bare before his hungry gaze. Outside our stall the women talk and talk, but all I care about is him and the crazy tumultuous heat swirling through my limbs.

His eyes lower as his fingers part me and I whimper. It's a small choked sound that I cannot help and the women pause in their chatter. I have no idea if we're discovered, but in that moment all I want is his mouth on me, drinking up the need I feel slipping from me.

Yes, Lucas, now, I beg silently.

And slowly he leans in.

His breath reaches me first, warm and teasing, and then the probe of his tongue. Its very tip flicks against my clit. I buck wildly, the whimper becoming a strangled squeal, and he breaks away, his eyes flashing in warning.

I bite into my lip so hard I fear I may draw blood. But the women continue with their chatter, and whether they've heard or not I don't care.

He leans back in and this time I'm ready for it, my body set rigid as I anticipate the spasm, the pleasure, the—

Oh, my fucking God.

* * *

She ripples beneath me, her muscles straining to keep still, and I can't help the smile that lifts my lips. How I've wanted this. Dreamt of it, even. Working her is a pleasure like none other.

Working her? My body mocks me. I am *drowning* in her. Her taste, her essence, her every reaction. She's working me. And I don't care.

I surround her perfect pussy, my nose nudging, my tongue dipping into the place I so want to plunge, and my cock swells harder, thicker, in the confines of my trousers.

She pants above me, her hands clawing at the counter. Everything about her urges me for more, to go faster, but I'm in my element…exploring, tasting, probing.

She shivers as I run my tongue over her clit, her breath a hiss between her teeth. I repeat the move, slow and hard at first, lapping at her. Jesus, I could stay like this for as long as she would let me. And then she writhes and I sense her climax building. I change my tempo, make quick flicks of my tongue in tune with her movements, then faster as she tenses.

I can't wait to tip her over and start anew. To feel her lose it and then go again and again.

I break away just enough to watch as I slip two fingers inside her, plunging deep and bringing them out wet and slick. She is so ready, so hot and needy, all for me.

I hear her pant my name. The sound mingles with the noise of my fingers inside her and with the muttering taking place outside the cubicle door and my smile grows. I want her to scream my name. I want her to forget her place, the perfect persona that she presents to the world, and break…*for me*.

I grow hungry…two fingers become three…and then her frenzied hands freeze, her knuckles flashing white at the counter-edge. I look up into her face, feasting on the desperate heat of her gaze, the fierce pinch of her teeth as she draws back her lower lip. I drop to her clit, sucking over her hard, and she cries out. The room stills but I don't stop. I can't stop. Not until she shatters under my hand, my mouth…

'Lucas… Lucas…'

I keep going, and then her thighs close around my head and her entire body convulses with wave after wave. She's coming hard and my body is at bursting point, living it with her. For a split second I worry I might lose it too—and then a cough breaks the air from the other side of the door. A prim, *what-do-you-think-you're-doing?* type of cough.

I look up at her, my grin as reckless as I feel, but something in her eyes holds me still, robbing me of breath. It's not their satiated blaze. There's something almost vulnerable—something that takes me back ten years.

And then she blinks. It's gone. Did I imagine it?

She releases the counter to comb her fingers through my hair. Her touch is like fire upon my skin and I shoot the thought down.

The heels outside retreat, the restroom door opens

and shuts. We're alone, and I'm not wasting the opportunity. I throw my focus back to her, leaning into her
warmth, her wetness, and I drink her down, cleaning
up every last drop.

She quivers around me, gives a small whimper.
'I'm…sensitive.'

I know she means in her body, the orgasm having
left her raw, but I think of that look. I need to replace
it with the wild heat of seconds before, so I soften my
touch upon her, I tease… I can feel her shifting away
from me, as if the moment is over, but I'm not ready.
I've not had my fill.

'We should be…getting back…before we're missed.'

Her words are hitched and I know I'm getting to her.
Her hand in my hair has turned rough, and her body
trembles with resurging tension.

'I can't…not again…not so soon.'

Wanna bet?

I hold her apart, my mouth and my tongue unrelenting. My body pleads for release. I know I should stand,
take her now. But I can't. I am lost to her pleasure.

'Oh, God, Lucas!'

This time she cries it so loud the sound echoes
through the empty room—hell, it probably reaches the
outer corridor too. This is madness. But I'm all for it.

She grips me against her with both hands now, her
hold fierce as her legs spread wide over the marble top.
She's clinging to me as if her life depends on it, but I'm
not going anywhere. I catch each wave of her orgasm

with my mouth. It's perfect, heavenly, and as I get to
my feet my cock spasms painfully.

Now.

I look down into her sparkling gaze. Her smile is
soft, warm.

'I didn't think—' She breaks off, her cheeks flushing deeper, her lashes lowering.

Her sudden embarrassment makes me ache—and
not with need, but with something I don't want to acknowledge. I use my hands to stroke her inner thighs
gently, holding her open to me. I don't know why I'm
waiting. I should bury myself in her and be done with
it. With this.

'It's a well-known fact that women can enjoy mul-
tiples.'

'In general—just not me.'

So I'm the first. That feeling swells inside me and I
drop my head. I need to kiss her. To taste those cherry-
red lips. But she turns her head away. It's a rejection.
A shot of ice water in my face.

'No kissing.'

'Fuck me, Evangeline, what we've just shared goes
a whole load further than kissing.'

Her thighs tense beneath my fingers and her palms
drop to my chest. 'I must get back.'

She has to be kidding.

Her hands forcing me away tell me otherwise.

I'm lost for words.

Carefully she closes her legs and slips from the countertop, bending to retrieve her thong from the floor. I

get there first. Scoop it up into my hand. Our gazes lock in silent challenge. Hell, if she's leaving me like this I'm taking *something*. Even if it's to reassure me that I didn't dream it.

She wets her lips, their glossy redness killing me. 'Fine—keep them.'

She smooths down her dress as she rises. I follow suit but make no attempt to leave. There's something about her I just can't shake. Call it too many years of absence, a need to make up for lost time, an opportunity to take what I've always wanted at last.

I have a ridiculous urge to say something—but what?

She reaches for the door latch and my hand covers hers on instinct. There are voices approaching once more and her eyes flicker in their general direction, away from me. I want so much to read her thoughts.

'You need to go, Lucas.'

Her voice is cold. Unsettling. And then she looks at me and I can't work out whether it's with hatred or sadness, or both. But it's enough for my hand to fall back to my side.

She pulls open the door, forcing me to move out of the way. It doesn't matter what her eyes tell me now. She wanted me—and that doesn't just die out on a simple tongue-fuck or two.

She turns to me, her hand hot against my chest as she backs me out of the cubicle.

'This isn't over,' I say.

But she smiles—it's soulless—and her hand shifts from me to curl around the edge of the cubicle door.

'Yes, it is... *Now* we're even.'

I register her meaning, shaking my head. *Like hell we are...*

'We're not even.' My grin is one of sheer arrogance. 'Not by a long shot.'

Her brow lifts into an elegant arch—I can't tell if it's in disbelief or challenge—and she closes the door in my face, the lock twisting into place.

It's a first for me. I should feel humiliated, cheapened—*used*, even. But I'm feeling none of those things.

Fire burns in my veins—fire for the chase, the thrill of the conquest. She will be mine. My groin pulses and I adjust myself, lifting my hand to sweep it over my face as determination settles in.

When I'm buried deep inside her—then we'll be even.

I turn and head for the door. I should clean up, but the lingering taste of her keeps me hungry. If I get my way, I'll have what I crave before the night is out.

And I *always* get my way.

CHAPTER THREE

I FEEL LIKE JELLY. It's the only way to describe how my insides tremble and my legs are weak.

Two orgasms.

Two.

I would have been content with one.

Whatever. You want more already—more a thousand times over.

And even then I know I'd still be wanting.

Because it could never just be about sex with him.

He's dangerous. To my senses, my sanity—and, if I really dwell on it, my heart. All over again.

I was foolish to even go there.

I circle the room, talking with prospective partners, my business persona enough to hide my distraction.

Him.

I feel his presence with every word I say, every breath I take, every clip of my heel against the gleaming floor as I walk. I can feel his eyes following me and I purposefully evade him. My schedule for the next two weeks is filling up and I know he'll be wanting his share. Perhaps that's why I leave him until last. Because I'm goading him. *Not* because I still want him.

He's at the bar now. I know it without looking. I've been aware of his movements ever since he appeared.

'Your feet aren't going to touch the ground over the next fortnight,' Clare tells me as she scans her tablet. 'And we still have those few that weren't able to make it tonight…'

He's moving. I can feel it.

Don't turn.

'I can offer them Friday,' she says, 'or later the following week. Of course, we still need to schedule in Waring Holdings, but if—'

'Good to see I'm on the radar.'

Shit. He's right behind me already.

I don't want him to know how I feel, and I don't want Clare to read it. So I school my expression, turning to face him with a polite smile that I hope masks a multitude of sins. I took what I wanted earlier to get him out of my system. I need him to see that. To hell with what my body is still saying.

'Of course you are, Lucas.' I gesture to Clare. 'My PA will arrange a convenient time for us to meet the week after next.' I add the timing for my own benefit, I need those days to get myself straightened out. 'Now, if you'll excuse me…?'

I move to leave but he steps in front of me, his frown so genuine I'm momentarily struck still.

'Does your PA deal with your after-hours schedule too?'

Now it's my turn to frown. He's not ready to let me

go. That much is obvious. 'Can you excuse us a second, Clare?'

'Sure.' She doesn't even quirk a brow at his remark, such is her professionalism, and I'm grateful for it.

I watch her walk away and purse my lips as I turn back to him. Refusing to acknowledge the excited tremble that runs up my spine as his eyes sparkle at me, glinting in the fairy lights adorning the tree beside us.

'Do you mind keeping this professional?'

If I expect my cold demeanour to rub off on him, it doesn't. He actually looks as if he's about to laugh.

'I was merely suggesting you might be hungry.'

His eyes trace a slow path to my belly and back up, teasing me through the silk.

'The hors d'oeuvres were delightful, but hardly enough to keep one going *all night*.'

I swallow. It's the way he draws out the words *all night*...the sequence of carnal images it paints...

'So, are you free for a late dinner? The place is emptying out.' His hand, still holding a glass, sweeps the room, but his eyes are all for me. 'For old times' sake, Evangeline. We've so much to catch up on.'

There's my name again. There's that same excited shudder. My brain is screaming at me to turn him down, to keep this all about business from here on in. It's wrong on so many levels—not least of all my family's. I want to be stronger. I want to be able to stamp this out and move on.

'Slow to work out that you're not wanted here, Waring?'

Shit. Dad.

I'd been so focused on Lucas I hadn't sensed my parents' approach. Now they're both standing directly beside me and I can feel the war building. This can't be happening. Not tonight of all nights. My night.

Fuck that.

A pulse moves in Lucas's jaw. He's mad. Really mad.

'I don't believe anyone has said that.' He raises his drink to his lips, the movement casual, but I can feel the barely restrained anger thrumming off his rigid stance.

My mother touches a hand to my father's arm. 'Now, David—'

'*I* am,' my father says, talking over her. 'And *she* will—won't you, Eva?'

He's looking at me. They both are. And I see red. This is what I've been fighting to escape—my family's control, interference, whatever you want to call it. For all that they love me, I'm tired of being under their thumb, dancing to their tune. And this is *my* product, *my* life. I've earned the right to say who I get involved with.

The way my brain phrases that last bit—*involved with*—isn't lost on me, but I push past it and look to my father.

'Waring Holdings is a good fit for the business.'

My father's colour deepens, his eyes widening as my mother's hand tightens upon his arm. But anger has given me the strength I need. Not just to deal with Dad, but with Lucas too.

'They will be on my list for consideration.'

I feel Lucas's chest puff and my eyes snap to his.

'Please ensure that Clare has your details before you

leave, so that we can arrange a mutually agreeable time to meet.'

My words leave no room for misunderstanding but rather than looking rebuked, he appears amused. The spark in his eye an open challenge. 'Of course.'

'Now, shall we go?' I say to my parents. 'We don't want to leave François waiting.'

My mother looks warily between us all. 'I thought you…?'

She's right. I told them before the night began that I wouldn't be joining them for dinner at their favourite French restaurant afterwards. I had some grand plan of a fancy takeaway, a hot bath and more champagne. Wallowing in my triumph, so to speak, and soaking away the stress of the last few months—years, even.

Now I know that a bath would only encourage debauched fantasies of what I might be doing with Lucas…

'I've changed my mind,' I say over the heat that starts to swirl, and I face him off. 'Thank you for coming, Lucas.'

His lip twitches and I read the double meaning in his eyes. Christ. I almost expect him to say, *Not me, but you did…twice.*

My cheeks flame as his eyes dance. 'I look forward to our next meeting.'

Look forward to it? I'll be on heat for it—*and* at my wits' end if I don't get this under control.

Still, I have at least a week—maybe more.

Plenty of time.

* * *

It's late when the door to Je l'adore opens and she emerges, her parents in tow.

I don't know why I'm here. Or rather I know why, but I don't approve of my actions.

Seems seeing her again has broken something in me. Something I kept locked away when I had a friendship to protect, a surrogate family to honour. Without it, I can't shake free.

I want to blame it on unsated desire. Sex. Simple as.

I tell myself that if I have her, then I can move on. It's an ability that's served me well in the past. I don't form attachments. Not any more.

I look at her now from my vantage point in the back of my limo across the street. She's laughing, her arms around her mother as they bid each other goodnight. There is so much love between them and my gut lurches at the sight of it. There'd been a time when I'd been part of that. Had loved and been loved, or so I'd thought.

Then she turns to her father and that lurch turns into a twist. I don't want to care any more. It's old ground. But I owe part of myself to that man, my only real father figure. He shaped me, and my success is in some way because of him.

Love, respect, anger—they all collide. I flex my fists, breathing through it. I always knew tonight would be hard, but there's so much I didn't bank on.

And right up there is this rush of feeling for her. An emotion I thought well and truly dead.

Seems she *is* my weakness after all.

She pecks her father on his cheek and I can almost sense his need to say something. I know him, and I know he's not going to let this go, but whatever he says she shakes her head at it and gestures for them to get in their waiting car.

I know she has an exclusive apartment around the corner—one of many homes owned by her family—and I'm banking on her heading back there tonight.

Just as I'm banking on getting what I came for...

I'm wired by the time I say goodbye to Mum and Dad. I could blame it on the amazing party—the culmination of my hard work. But it's not. It runs a whole lot deeper.

Loving Lucas had been as natural as breathing in my teens. And just as impossible to prevent. He'd always been a part of our lives, his mother constantly using mine as a sitter so she could go on date after date, never finding anyone permanent.

I don't know whether she was picky or desperate, but it had made me mad. Mad at how she could neglect Lucas, not care about him. The day he got his exam results I remember her delivering a swift 'well done, honey' before planting a kiss on his forehead and leaving for the night. There was no celebration—no nothing.

It had been my parents who had cheered him on, congratulating him, spoiling both him and Nate because they'd done well.

We'd even taken him away with us on family holidays. It had been inevitable, really.

He'd been gorgeous, athletic and toned, intelligent, a rebel, but never taking it too far—not like Nate, who never knew when to quit. It was always Lucas reining him in, looking out for him.

He'd looked out for me too, and my heart had revelled in it. Loving the way he didn't disregard my opinion, unlike Dad and Nate, who saw me as just a girl. Lucas made me feel special.

But when his mother had died suddenly things changed. We truly became his family, gave him a home, and as much as Nate was his best friend, and my father a man he respected and could call on for advice, my mother the one to feed, water and look after him, I was Lucas's ear. It was my turn to be there for him.

I was the one he talked to about how he felt, about his grief which was tainted with guilt at not having been the closest of sons to his mother. But his remorse only succeeded in making me more angry, more protective, as I tried to tell him it wasn't his fault. She should've been a better mother. She should've been there for him more.

Like I had been.

Until my eighteenth birthday, that is. Until I pushed him too far.

I was naïve to think he would consider me worth the risk. Naïve to think he could have loved me enough.

I take a shaky breath and duck my head against the bitter cold wind. I know better now. I won't go there again.

I teeter down the pavement towards home and I

shiver. The champagne topped up with wine had been doing a fine job of warding off the chill until now.

How could things have gone so wrong five years ago?

Ten years ago I messed up and he broke my heart.

But five years ago, he and Nate and their business… I just don't get it.

My parents loved Lucas—*Nate* loved him. I can't believe he just bailed on the company, as my father and Nate claim. They hate him for it, but the Lucas I know—I *knew*—wouldn't do that. And the anger, the resentment—it's there on both sides.

If we're to work together I need to get the full story. I need to know I can trust him. Which means I need Lucas to tell me his side of it. And that means dragging up the past.

I wanted to press Dad at dinner, to be honest and tell him that I suspect Nate of playing a greater role in what went down five years ago. But I didn't. Instead, Lucas just became the elephant in the room.

A rather sexy, irresistible, *fuck-me-now* elephant.

I remember how he looked on his knees, his head buried between my legs, and the chill evaporates with a lick of heat. I wonder whether his trunk would be just as impressive as the oversized animal's…

A surprised laugh erupts over my crazed thoughts.

'You know, talking to oneself is the first sign of madness.'

Lucas. Oh, God.

I misstep and quickly correct it. Straightening my

spine I turn to face him, praying that the low light hides the excitement rising beneath my shock. 'Technically, I was laughing, and *that* is a sign of good character... not that you'd know much about that.'

His brow lifts over eyes that flicker and I wonder if my words sting. Guilt fires inside me—*it's a low blow*—but I bury it.

'What are you doing here, Lucas?'

'I would have thought that was obvious.'

I take a shaky breath and remind myself of the trillion reasons why this needs to stop. 'I thought I made it clear earlier that we're even.'

He steps towards me and heat flares with his proximity. My lungs drag in air that is tainted with his cologne.

'And I told *you*,' he murmurs, 'we're not...not even close.'

I hear the desire ring in his voice, feel it echo in my blood, and I force myself to turn away, to walk. 'It's close enough, Lucas.'

'That's not what your eyes were telling me earlier, Evangeline.'

He follows close behind me and I ignore the shiver of delight, wrapping my arms around my middle, hugging my faux fur coat tight.

I can't tell him that I'm scared of falling for him again. But I can tell him that my family hating him makes this a very bad idea.

But part of me suspects he is doing this *because* of my family and their vendetta.

I know my product is good enough to warrant his attention, but *this*—this has nothing to do with my product and everything to do with me.

'Are you denying that you want me?'

I can hear the disbelief in his voice and it annoys me. Like my father—like my brother, even—he assumes he knows what I want. Is he going to start dictating what's best for me too?

'No, I think you know that well enough,' I admit. There's no point in lying about the obvious. 'You knew it ten years ago and you know it all over again now. But here's the thing, Lucas…'

I turn to face him. My apartment is a building away now. Sanctuary is close. I just need to hold it together a few more moments.

'I'm not the kid I was then. I won't jeopardise my work for some…' I struggle for the right phrase and settle for the easiest, most innocent. 'Some silly distraction.'

His laugh is low, seductive, and he takes advantage of my stationary state to close the distance between us, reaching out his hand to cup my jaw. I want to move away, to stop the frisson at his touch, but I can't make my body obey.

His thumb is soft, warm as he brushes it over my cheekbone, and my eyes are lost in the darkness of his, so close I can just make out the rim of brown, the flecks of gold that dance in the snow-white lights adorning the trees that line the street.

'There's nothing silly about the way I feel right now.'

Dammit, does he have to look so sincere?

A group of revellers round the corner and start moving down the street, their voices deep and loud as they roll out a rendition of 'Good King Wenceslas'.

'Seems we're destined to have spectators,' he says.

And as my lips part on no words I'm swamped by the memory of our previous encounter and the fear that I want him to kiss me. So much it hurts. But it'll be my undoing. A ten-year-old memory stoked, refreshed, and my feelings with it.

And a hope for something that just isn't possible.

My tongue sweeps across my lower lip.

It's nerves. I'm just nervous.

My clit pangs painfully, mocking me.

'Please, Lucas, this has to stop.'

I think of his mouth, his tongue, the dizzying pressure he administered so expertly over me. *Stop. Don't stop.* My thoughts are as chaotic as the blood racing through my veins.

'Tell me to leave…'

He steps forward, close enough to stop the chill wind breaching the gap between us, and now I'm just hot. Hot and confused.

'…and I will.'

'I…I…'

'*Tell* me.'

'Please…' I try again and fail. I don't want to breathe—don't want to inhale his scent, his warmth, his appeal. All my barriers are collapsing.

'Evangeline…'

My name rolls over his tongue and his head dips.

The air sits in my lungs as I neither rebuke him nor pull him in. And then he sweeps past my mouth, along my cheek to my ear, his lips gently brushing over my skin with his words.

'I want you.'

A strange whimper sounds, and as he lifts his head, his lips curving, I know it's come from me. I see the triumph in his gaze as he moves for my mouth and a slice of sanity erupts.

'Don't kiss me.'

I palm his chest and he frowns.

'Don't make this about more than sex.'

His head tilts to one side as he studies me, the meaning of my words sinking in. 'Last time I checked, kissing was quite an essential element—quite an irresistible element.'

He looks to my mouth, eyes hungry, and as though emphasising his point he runs his teeth over his lower lip. *God, yes.* My tummy contracts on a rush.

'Oi-oi! Get yourself a room!' one of the passing revellers declares, and there's a string of cheers and laughter from his crew.

Lucas doesn't flinch—doesn't even back away. 'A room sounds like a good idea to me.'

He reaches around me with his other hand and brings me closer. Close enough to feel his hardness pressing between us. Damn suits and their forgiving cloth. I didn't need any confirmation of his impressive trunk. Not when I'm hanging by a thread.

My hands soften against him. 'This isn't a good idea.'

'*Au contraire.* I see it as the only way to get our business off on the right foot.'

He leans back in, his mouth hovering by my ear once more.

'I need to know how it feels to be inside you…to cease the raging fantasy and know the real thing. I need to know so I don't spend every meeting thinking about what it would be like to bend you over and fuck you hard.'

Air flutters past my lips. I could come just listening to his dirty talk. No one has ever spoken to me like this. No one.

'Lucas…'

It's not his name that betrays my every want. It's the husky intonation, the plea-like quality of my voice. I don't care that the revellers are now wolf-whistling and cheering, entertained by our display.

My body surrenders and my lashes close… 'Your room or mine?'

CHAPTER FOUR

SHE OPENS HER eyes and for a second, I wonder if she will still refuse me.

Something vulnerable, something edgy persists in her gaze, but then she turns and walks away.

No refusal, then...

I follow.

She hasn't told me to go. She hasn't told me to stay.

But one thing I'm sure of, Evangeline does what she wants and I'll go along with it until she tells me otherwise.

Hell, I don't want this to be about more than sex either. It will only muddy the waters, exposing us both to a future headache neither of us needs.

But not kissing her?

That's like being gifted a three-course dinner without the main course.

And those lips...

She turns to look at me now as she pushes the door open and holds it for me. They curve a little and her lashes lower as I step forward. I want to taste them... to feel them part beneath my pressure...to swallow her moan with the one I know I'd give.

Because I've only tasted them once, and the memory is burned into my soul.

She says nothing as we cross the harsh white vestibule. It's all glass, high ceilings and bright lights, but she lifts its starkness just by being there and I can't look away.

A warning sparks in my gut—a warning I want to ignore.

So much time has passed since I loved her. The sweet, feisty, fun-loving girl that she was. So many women have come and gone since, none of whom have inspired a need for more or warranted a trust I feel incapable of giving. I date. I have fun. I move on. They're not relationships as such. Merely acquaintances who satisfy the basic urge for companionship, sex.

I want it to be the same with her. Safe.

But it's not.

I had so much to lose back then and it served me well, kept me protected.

But now there are no barriers against what's burning between us, and I should be running the other way.

But I'm not.

We reach the lift and she presses the button to call it. I half expect her to turn, tell me she's changed her mind, but she doesn't and the warning starts to trickle through my spine: *Are you sure you can keep a lid on this?*

She sneaks a look at me from beneath her lashes, her thoughts hidden as she nibbles over her lip—that deliciously full lip that I want to trace with my tongue—and a tide of longing drowns out the panic.

The lift opens and we walk in. It's vacant and small. I expected it to be vast, to give me room to stave off the heat her nearness is driving. I've wanted her for so long. Fantasised about it even when I knew I shouldn't. And now I'm going to have her I want it to last—not to erupt like my teenage self would have done.

But it's impossible to put down the semi-permanent erection I've been sporting since sitting between her legs. Hell, even before then. From the moment she gave me that look across the room, daring me to follow her. It was there with her intent, her desire.

I fist my hands inside my pockets, fix my gaze to the lift doors and count to ten…twenty… The ground shifts to a gentle stop. The top floor. The penthouse. Only the best for the Beaumonts.

As the doors slide open there's more white, more glass, more coldness. It's similar to my place, further into the city, but it reeks of her family—not her. Not the girl I knew. But as for the woman… What do I truly know?

We should have gone to mine.

'You don't like it?'

I realise she's caught me frowning, my hands still deep in my pockets and my shoulders tense. I force myself to relax and give her a smile. 'It's not what I expected.'

She shrugs off her coat and opens a concealed closet, hanging it up. 'It's my parents' place, and it's *exactly* how they like it.'

'Not you.'

It's a simple statement, and I guess I could be wrong but I want to know I'm right. I see a flash of colour run along her cheekbones, her lips twitching.

Not only am I right, I've pleased her—and, Christ, does it feel good.

'No, not really.' She closes the closet and starts to head off towards an open living space. 'I have a place I'm renovating in Notting Hill. This is a stopgap.'

My smile grows with my confidence as I follow her. I still *know* her. 'What colour?'

She eyes me over her shoulder as she enters the kitchen and reaches for a glass. 'Colour?'

'The house…'

She gives a soft laugh. 'What makes you think I've gone for a colour?' she asks, dispensing water from the sleek black fridge door. 'I could have gone for *au naturel* stone.'

She leans back against the countertop and takes a sip from the glass, her eyes holding mine.

'Again…not you.'

She smiles approvingly. 'Pink.'

'Pink?'

My brow rises—she *has* to be teasing. I search her gaze and it dances with humour. I would have had her saying blue—yellow, even—but *pink*…

'Now you look like my mother when I told her the same.'

I laugh as I imagine the scene and see humour reflected in her gaze. She looks beautiful, amused, so at ease suddenly, and it warms me through. It feels like old times. When the banter was so quick to spark between us.

I smile. 'I bet she was all for yellow—am I right?'

'Yellow, or even blue, anything but pink.'

She shakes her head softly and there's a silent exchange, an acceptance that we still *work*.

I can feel it.

And then it's gone.

She stiffens as the mood shifts and I grapple to get it back. 'Whatever floats your boat, I say.'

She takes a breath, visibly composing herself as she turns away to place her glass on the side.

'You do,' she says, her eyes coming back to me, her voice low, her eyes intent. 'Right now.'

The swift change from light-hearted to sexual unsettles me. My eyes narrow. Is she forcing us back to sex? Taking away our connection? The personal talk?

You should be happy.

She gives her head a small flick as her eyes stare into mine. 'Or have you changed your mind?'

Fuck that.

I'm moving before I know it.

Fuck personal. Fuck talk.

She's in my arms, her hands beneath my jacket shoving it down my shoulders. I throw it to one side, pulling her back against me and seeking out her mouth, instinct driving me, making me forget not to kiss her. She turns away, arching her neck and offering up the creamy expanse of skin instead.

The gesture cuts deep and I scrape my teeth against

her—a nip of punishment and acceptance in one—
and the whimper it draws triggers a groan of my own.
Christ. The series of things I want to do to her, *with* her,
is rampaging through my brain, and my arousal strains
painfully between us.

I run my hands over her dress, seeking out the fastening—a zipper, buttons, anything. It's frustrating as
hell. 'If you don't get this off, I swear I'm going to rip it.'

She laughs at me. The husky lilt driving me crazy.

'So impatient...'

'I've had ten years to wait for this. I call that pa-
tience enough.'

Her eyes widen as she stares up at me and she's momentarily still.

Shit. Too much.

'Off,' I command, wanting her back in the moment,
to forget what I said.

And she turns away to pull the escaped curls over her
shoulder. 'The zipper is concealed in the back.'

I find the fastening and slowly—too slowly for
my tortured cock, but too quickly for my struggling
control—I lower it, exposing her exquisite skin, her
spine that I want to trace with my fingers, my lips, my
tongue. Goosebumps prickle where the fabric parts,
calling to me, and I press a kiss to the nape of her neck,
breathing her in.

'You are beautiful, Evangeline.'

She shudders on a breath, turning her head so that
I'm on the periphery of her vision, her lashes low, her
forbidden lips parted. The zipper stops over the curve

of her bare arse and I remember her thong sitting pretty in my pocket. I smile. She went to dinner like this, bare and exposed, thanks to *me*.

And then all sane thought leaves me as she slips the dress from her shoulders and it pools at her feet. Her perfectly round cheeks are exposed to my hungry gaze and I can't breathe, can't move, can't believe.

Her eyes lift to mine above her shoulder. 'Are you just going to stare?'

'I'm savouring.'

Engraving this moment in my memory, worshipping it—you, Evangeline.

I reach out to smooth each mound and she curves into my touch, her teeth biting into her lip.

'Please, Lucas, I want you now. You can savour later.'

Later? How much later? In an hour? Two? A day? A week?

I don't pose the question; the answer is too depressing.

And if I only get to be inside her once, I'm going to make it the best she's ever known.

I bow my head into the curve of her neck, my lips gently brushing her skin as I say, 'Now who's impatient, hmm…?'

I grasp her hips and pull her back against my clothed erection, relishing the moan she gives in return, the feel of her cheeks cradling my arousal. And when I release her to trail my fingers up her sides she doesn't move away. She stays curved against me, her palms planted on the cold white countertop as she pushes into me.

I lift my lips to the edge of her ear. 'What would your parents say to you fucking in their kitchen?'

She whimpers—she likes my dirty talk. I know it and I love her for it.

Enough with the love!

I focus on my hands. I want to touch her everywhere, claim her everywhere, coax out every sound of ecstasy she's capable of making. I stroke along her back and unclasp her bra. The nude lace obediently falls open, the straps landing loose down her arms before I encourage them off. Her breasts fall free. I can't see them, but knowing they are there, waiting, has me aching, painful, *desperate*.

I trace the curve of her waist around to her belly, higher... I stroke beneath the curve of her breasts, feel their weight shift as she writhes.

'God, Lucas, *please*.'

I grit my teeth against her heated plea, feel my control fraying as I rotate my palms and surround each breast. I shudder on my own breath even as I feel her do the same, feel her hardened beads pressing into my palms. I roll her nipples between my thumbs and forefingers, making them harder, prouder, feeling the tautness in the ripples that surround them.

Just perfect.

Perfect and mine.

For now.

I pinch them tighter and she inhales sharply between her teeth.

'God, *yes*.'

'You like that?'

My voice is strained, my balls heavy. I'm so close, and I know she is too.

'Yes...'

It's practically a hiss as she leans back, her body arched. Her bra hits the floor as she flicks it away so she can raise her hands to my neck, and I do it again and again, making her writhe. Her naked body against my clothed one. It's one hell of a contrast and it's pushing me over.

I'm tempted to make her come like this. It's clear she would. But I need to feel her—feel her wetness, the evidence of her need.

I trail one hand down her belly and she sucks her tummy in.

'I can't get your pussy out of my head,' I tell her, kissing her shoulder. 'The way you taste...' I nip her skin. 'The way you move...' She claws my neck as I cup her and her legs shift apart, granting me all the access I need. 'The way you're wet just for me...'

I move, sliding my middle finger in deep, and pull back until her clit is beneath my fingertip. Slowly I rotate it over her and she whimpers, the noise sending my balls heavenward. The smooth undulation of her hips is pushing my release and I grit my teeth.

Not yet.

I'm losing it.

It's the only way to explain how we've got to this point. In my parents' perfect, clinical abode. All orderly and cold. Me naked. Him clothed. Me on the brink. Him…

Oh, yes…

I can feel he's close. Every taut muscle is pressing into my back, and his stance as he rocks with rigid precision against me is so fucking hot. I ride my arse against him, staving off my own release.

I want him to come. I want him to come inside his clothing. I want to feel that power—to know that a man like Lucas Waring can lose it, still caged inside his underwear, over *me*. It's that which keeps me just this side of sane.

I drop one hand to move it with his and feel his body jerk.

'Christ, Evangeline.' His breath rasps. 'What are you *doing* to me?'

I smile through the salacious heat whipping around us, pushing his fingers lower, encouraging him to sink inside me as I move with him.

He breathes into my neck, his stubble grazing my skin as he buries his face there. His other hand drops to my thigh and grabs it, lifting it, granting himself greater access, greater friction over my clit as his wrist rubs against me and his cock presses harder, more urgently.

'Yes, Lucas, yes…' I pant, and my control is slipping.

But his is too. He's trembling against me, his body ever more tense, and then I am gone. Wave after wave crashes over me, and my head is swimming with ecstasy. And then I feel him, hear his growl into my shoulder, feel his teeth biting as he bucks and shudders, his own release wild and sudden.

I hang off his neck, holding him to me, keeping us locked together, and my lips stretch in a triumphant smile. I look to the pristine white ceiling, catch our reflection in the rim of a chrome spotlight, and it's a reminder that this is *real*. So very real and so electrifying.

I should be scared—scared of what it means for the future, scared about whether I can give this up. Instead I'm content in his arms, naked and at home.

'Fuck, I haven't… I shouldn't have…'

He shakes his head and his disbelief, his sudden vulnerability, resonates through me. I turn and hook my hands behind his neck, eager to see off any hint of real emotion—because *that* I can't deal with.

'Oh, yes, you should…because *that* was erotic as fuck.'

He lifts his lashes; his eyes meet mine and I am winded. They are almost shy as they search, seeking out a lie that doesn't exist. It *was* fucking hot. It was everything I wanted.

'You have to be kidding me…?' His hands drop to my behind, soft, yielding.

He doesn't believe me.

'No.'

I almost kiss him—can feel the urge burning through my veins. But where would that leave us?

And then his crazy statement replays in my mind: *'I've had ten years to wait for this.'*

Shit.

I push it away. I can't think about what that means. It's too hopeful. And I learned my lesson once. I won't go there again. *Focus on the sex.* It's tangible. It's what he came for and it's the one thing I agreed to and can give. For tonight.

'Just thinking about it turns me on all over again,' I say.

As if on cue my nipples prickle into his shirt and I run my teeth over my lower lip. I'm not kidding. Three orgasms and still I want more. I know it's a bad sign, but as I curve into him, breathing him in, I couldn't care less.

Slowly his smile lifts, his eyes with it, and he presses his forehead to mine. 'Keep talking like that and I'll be taking you to bed next.'

'I like the sound of that…' I smile, all sultry. 'But how about a shower first?'

I take his hand and before I can question my senses I head to the bathroom, loving how he comes with me. No question. No hesitation. This feels like a dream.

One that I don't want to wake up from.

Again, it's a warning. Again, I ignore it, pushing open the bedroom door and heading straight for the en suite bathroom.

Lucas releases my hand and I look at him over my shoulder.

'I'm stripping for this,' he says.

Then it hits me—we've done so much but I've not seen him naked. *Not yet.*

I reach into the bathroom to set the shower going before sauntering towards him. He's placing his cufflinks on the dressing table that blends into the shelving system that runs along one wall. His dark, erotic presence is at total odds with the crisp white room. He doesn't belong here. Hell, neither do I. But it only makes my blood rush faster, my ache build.

He's tugging his tie undone when I reach him, and I go to work on his shirt, pulling it out of his trousers and moving on to the buttons. My eyes follow my progress, and my mouth dries further the more skin I unveil, the more muscle, the more toned ripples that are triggered with each scrape of my fingers.

I've seen him shirtless before. He only ever slept in lounge pants when he stayed with us. And he was captivating then—in a boyish, trim way. But now he's all hard, lean muscle and I can't believe I'm getting to strip him.

'I've waited ten years for this...'

His voice reverberates through my mind. Ten years ago he refused me, and didn't give me a backward glance. Or so I thought. Now he's hinting at something else…something more.

My insides twist. My heart aches. I want this to be about sex. I don't want to feel anything else—not on that level.

'Hey, are you okay?'

I realise I've stilled, my eyes unseeing on his chest, my fingers frozen.

You fool.

'Of course,' I say softly, pressing a kiss to his chest

and breathing in the thought-obliterating scent of him as I tell my brain to shut down. To go with the flow.

I release the last button and smooth my hands over his shoulders, coaxing off his shirt, exposing the beauty of him to my appreciative gaze. He really is exquisite. I've had men—of course I have. I almost married one in trying to forget Lucas.

That foolish move seems ever more idiotic as I drown in a sea of sensation over the man before me now.

I could never forget Lucas. Never carve him out of me.

I trace his pecs, watch them flicker, then I lick my lips as I trail my hands lower, over the taut expanse of muscle to the hint of hair that thickens above his belt buckle.

I move to unfasten his trousers and he catches my wrists, halting me. I look up, questioning, praying I can hide the swirl of emotion running away inside me.

'As much as you found it a turn-on,' he says with a lopsided smile, 'I'm taking myself in there and getting these off alone.'

He steps around me and I watch him go, mesmerised by the movement of his shoulder blades, by the sharp waist and the curve of his behind in those trousers.

Fuck, how I want to bite that.

I giggle at my own crazed desire. It's so unlike me. As if a dormant part has suddenly awakened inside of me and is taking over. Pushing out all else.

Thank God.

I give him a minute, until I hear the sound of the

water change, and then I know he is in there…ready and waiting.

I go in. My sanity well and truly gone. There'll be time for that tomorrow. I need him inside me now… filling me, making me whole.

I enter the cubicle and he's there, slicked up, his eyes dark and needy. I step forward and my smart-watch beeps. I don't know why I look at it. Maybe it's because he does. But I immediately wish I hadn't.

The incoming text message glares up at me, and with it everything changes.

I can't *un*-see it.

I wish I could. But I can't.

I should be grateful. But I'm not.

CHAPTER FIVE

FIVE DAYS SINCE I've seen her.

Five days since she told me to finish my shower and leave.

I'd blame it on the fact that I lost my load like an inexperienced fool if not for the fact she was so turned on by it. She told me so herself and I believed her. It was written on her face...in her actions.

And then her watch beeped and she morphed into someone else entirely.

A cold replica.

She had no time for me...for *us*.

Not that there would ever *be* an 'us'—but, hell, in that moment in her kitchen...before, during, after...I felt things shift between us. I thought it felt *right*, picking up where we'd left off ten years prior, saying to hell with everyone and everything else.

Clearly I was wrong.

She offered no explanation. Nothing. As if I didn't even warrant one. And I wasn't about to give her the satisfaction of grovelling for justification.

I cleaned up, dressed and left.

Two days later Monday morning hit, and my PA informed me that my meeting with her had been scheduled for a week Friday.

I laughed. Actually laughed. Did she really think she could keep me hanging on for two weeks like some insignificant prospect?

But you've only got yourself to blame.

I've hardly covered myself in glory, following her around like some fool, giving her the impression she can wrap me around her little finger.

But no more.

It's time she saw the real me. The one who stays in control.

So now I'm here, in her building, more than a week early and ready to face the music.

I know she's not going to like this, but I have a score to settle. Not just professionally, but personally too.

'Mr Waring, I'm afraid Miss Beaumont has an appointment with Houston Logistics right now,' her PA says to me, her smile polite but confused. 'I believe we have an appointment scheduled for next week on Friday?'

I give her a smile loaded with charm. 'That *was* the case, but Houston and I have decided to swap.'

'To…swap?'

Her brows lift past the rim of her thick black glasses and I want to laugh. It's a worrying sign. Laughter tells me that I'm nervous. And I'm never nervous.

Control, Lucas. Control.

I clear my throat and slot my hands into my pockets,

letting my eyes drift across the office and back to her.
'That's right. We—'

'Lucas?'

Eva.

My pulse skips a beat. Her sudden presence triggers
an adrenaline shot and I'm slow to turn to face her, to
neutralise it.

'Evangeline, it's good to see you.'

Good? Christ. 'Good' has nothing on the reality.

She's striking in pink today. A simple shirt that looks
anything but simple clings to her curves and disappears
into a tight black skirt. Her legs are exposed from the
knee down and accentuated by heels that trigger a carnal hit, making me think about things that have no place
in this room right now.

Control.

I drag my eyes back up to her hair—something innocent. It's twisted high on her head, smart and professional and sexy as fuck.

Dammit all.

I meet her eyes. They're bright. Their blue depths
alive and popping. I could say it was down to effective
make-up, but I know it's her reaction to me.

And then I find my control. I'm not alone in this.
She feels it too.

It puts us on an even footing, at least.

My chest eases and I step forward, offering my hand.
She eyes it suspiciously before taking it for the briefest
handshake I've ever experienced. But I feel the current

that sparks between us, and I see it reflected in her dilated gaze as she looks up at me.

'I'm afraid I'm too busy to see you today.' She crosses her arms, her lips giving a delightful little tremble as she breathes. 'If you'd called ahead we could have saved you the disappointment.'

She looks past me to her PA.

'Clare, when are Mr Waring and I scheduled to meet?'

'Well, you—'

'Now.' I cut over her. There's no point dragging this out. 'Shall we…?'

I gesture to the open door behind her. Her office. But she's busy looking at her PA, as though she needs saving, and I allow myself a momentary sense of satisfaction because I've unsettled her.

It doesn't beat my experience last Friday night. No, I had the rug well and truly pulled out from beneath me then. But it's a start.

'It seems Mr Waring and Houston Logistics have made an arrangement to swap appointment slots.'

I almost feel sorry for her PA as her voice pitches, and I know she can sense the undercurrent between us.

'Swap?' Eva looks at me incredulously. 'Clare, could you ring and confirm that's the case?'

'Sure.'

'No need—use my mobile.' I extract my phone. 'Houston's in my recently dialled—we played in a golf tournament Sunday. Great chap.'

'Of course you did.'

She doesn't take my phone—she doesn't spare me another glance. She simply turns on her heel and starts for her office.

'Clare, would you mind bringing me a coffee, please?'

Something tells me she wants something stronger than coffee, and I have to stop myself from grinning.

'No problem.' Her PA looks at me, hesitant. 'Can I get you one too, Mr Waring?'

I force my attention off Eva's elegant curves as she strides away—she's so damn sexy when she's pissed off. 'Black, no sugar. Thank you,' I say, and follow her in.

Her office is contemporary. A geometric pattern adorns the grey walls, but there are splashes of colour everywhere. Splashes of her. It has a bright couch with co-ordinating chairs, and a glass coffee table adorned with industry magazines. Her desk is large, a mixture of modern glass and old twisted oak. Interesting, fascinating...just as its owner.

I close the door behind me and wait for her to offer me a seat. Actually, I'm waiting for the eruption that I sense is coming.

She's standing at the room's only window, looking out. From here, I can't make out what she sees, but I'm guessing it's the park across the road. Her building is in a residential area of the city—it's pleasant. Especially on a day like today, when the sun is out, not a cloud in sight.

Her shoulders lift as she takes a long, drawn-out

breath. 'It's a shame you didn't have the decency to let me know about your little arrangement with Houston.'

Her voice is brittle. As if I've done something to offend her. As if it's me who kicked *her* out and not the other way around. My teeth grind.

Control, Lucas. Today is about business.

Except it's not.

If it was purely work I would have left it until next week to prove my company's worth. Instead I'm here now, trying to push past Friday night.

'An oversight—my apologies.'

My tone is careful, restrained, and she turns to me.

If looks could kill...

'I like to feel prepared for my meetings, don't you?' she asks.

She has a point. 'Of course.'

She walks to her desk and wakes up her computer. 'Then you'll understand my request to rearrange.'

I laugh before I can stop it and her eyes flash to me.

'Something funny?'

'Look, I'm here with the perfect deal, tailored to your product—there's nothing you need to prepare. Unless...'

I look at her—really look at her. The quick undulation of her chest is giving away her rapid breath, and there's a persistent flush to her skin. I had it tagged as annoyance, but now I'm not so sure.

I close the distance between us and she backs up, her eyes widening. 'What is it, Evangeline? Did you want more time in the hope that whatever this is between us would go away?'

She scoffs and looks back to her screen. 'So bloody full of yourself, aren't you?'

I raise my hands in defence. 'You're the one acting all angry. A simple switch in meetings shouldn't warrant this. Although, let's be honest, it's me who got the brutal rejection—a naked one at—'

'Stop it, Lucas.'

'What? Reminding you of the truth? Of what we were about to do before that—'

'Look, you want to talk business? Fine. Let's do that.'

She drops into a seat and gestures for me to do the same. She won't look at me, though, and I'm itching to push my luck, to walk around her desk and lift her chin, force her to accept it's still there, riding strong.

'But stick to business, Lucas, or you're out.'

I move to the seat she's offered me and stand before it. 'Just tell me one thing...' I shouldn't ask, and part of me doesn't want to know, but... 'What changed?'

She looks up at me, eyes hesitant, the bob of her throat giving her away. 'I don't know what you mean.'

'You do know what I mean. One minute we're having the best sex of our lives...' I see her entire body clench, her fingers fisting over her keyboard, and I know she's fighting it—fighting the heat the memory triggers. 'The next your watch tells you something and you turn into an ice queen... So what gives?'

She closes her eyes, her fingers relaxing over the keys, and I can't bear it. She's shutting me out and I want to know why.

'Or should the question be—*who*?'

Her lashes lift. Her eyes are unreadable—hatefully unreadable. There was a time I could have read her like a book, but this new skill she has is driving me crazy. All the more so because I'm letting it get to me.

'That has no place in this conversation.'

'Are you sure about that?'

'Positive.'

She looks at her phone and activates the screen, calm as the day outside. 'I have another meeting this afternoon, so I suggest we get on with this.'

I feel my mouth gape and quickly snap it shut.

'I'll find out what's keeping Clare first.'

She stands and leaves. Her absence is just as frustrating as her presence.

'That has no place in this conversation...'

That makes the reason personal. And if it's personal, does that mean she has another man? Was it guilt that had her kicking me out?

I can't believe it of her. The Eva I know wouldn't be unfaithful, no matter how strong our connection. But if it's not another man...

I look to her phone on the desk. Whatever that notification was, there'll be a record of it on there. The temptation to lift it and take a chance on it being unlocked, or possessing an easy-to-guess PIN is there, but I'm not going to sink that low. I'm not.

As if I've summoned it, the phone starts to flash with an incoming call: *Nate.*

Something twists deep inside me and I feel I have my answer.

She took me back to her place straight off the back of seeing her parents. Their hold over her wasn't enough to stop it. *But Nate...*

My lip curls; the bitter, acrid taste of betrayal stings my throat.

I let him get between us before, there's no way I'll let it happen again.

This contract was important enough when it was purely business—now it just got personal, *real* personal, and I'll do everything within my power to see it signed. Pull every trick in the book if I have to.

She *will* sign it.

And do a whole lot more if I have my way.

The business is revenge enough, but Eva... She's the icing on the cake.

As I walk back into my office, I notice two things that stop me in my tracks.

Firstly, Lucas has made himself at home, and I don't want to feel the excited rush that comes with the sight. His jacket is slung over the back of his chair and he has his laptop propped open as he taps away, his crisp white shirt rippling with the movement of his shoulders, his hair falling forward over his forehead.

Too appealing. Too comfy.

Secondly, my phone has moved. It now sits alongside his laptop and my eyes rest there as my heart lurches.

Has he...? Could he have...? It's my birthdate—would he remember?

He turns his head to look at me, but barely acknowledges my presence before he looks back to his screen and slides my phone across the desk, to where it was before.

'It kept ringing, so I silenced it.'

I come alive at his voice—so matter-of-fact, so deep and thrilling. 'Right. Sorry.'

Jesus. Why am I apologising? I remember the coffees I'm holding on to and kick the door closed behind me before striding over and slapping one down next to him.

'It's not quite barista standard but it does the job well enough.'

'Thank you.'

His lashes lift but I don't wait for our eyes to meet—not at this proximity. Not even excusing myself on the pretence of chasing up Clare has helped me get my head back in the game. I quickly scoot to my side of the desk, putting a whole chunk of glass and wood between us. Better.

'Don't you want to see who's been calling? They've been quite persistent.'

He doesn't look at me as he asks the question but there's an edge to his tone—something that has my skin prickling.

'It can wait.'

Now he looks at me and his eyes are cold, piercing. 'You sure about that?'

I swallow. 'Yes.'

'I think you should at least check.'

He's goading me, and I don't want to give him the satisfaction, but I can't stop curiosity getting the better of me. I reach out and activate the screen, glancing at it with my trusty poker face. Not that I think it will fool him.

Three missed calls. Nate.

Shit.

I shut the screen down and lean back in my chair, taking my coffee with me. 'I'll call him back later.'

'Three missed calls, though,' he pushes. 'Could be urgent?'

I give a dismissive shrug and his eyes lower briefly, burning into the fabric of my blouse. It's buttoned high, it's perfectly decent, and yet I feel as if he's stripped me. Heat swamps my belly, my breasts, my nipples prickle against the lace of my bra.

'It's fine. I'll call him back later.'

I'm repeating myself, but this time the words are harder, stronger, fed with the strength of will it's taking for me to fight this dogged attraction. Because that's all this can be—attraction. I don't know Lucas now, and I don't know the truth of what went down five years ago with Nate, or the true reason he is back. I want to think it's for my product, but is it really?

He gives me a slow smile and closes the lid of his laptop. 'Okay.'

I watch him take up his coffee, watch him sip at the hot, steaming liquid, and not once does he release me from his gaze. *I* could look away, but it feels like a challenge: first who does admits defeat.

Well, not me...

'Shall I start from the top?' he asks. 'Me? My company? The basics? Or is that a bit like covering old ground?'

How is he doing it? Remaining so calm when I know he's not? He wanted me to see that Nate had called. He wanted to test me…assess my reaction. Has he worked out it was Nate who ruined Friday too?

'I know enough about Waring Holdings,' I say, grateful for my projected confidence.

'Is that so?' He shoots me a grin as he settles back in his seat. 'Please enlighten me.'

I wonder if this is a test too, or if he's genuinely curious as to what I know.

I humour him, reeling off facts and figures, cities of presence, high-profile partners—the lot—and I know I've surprised him. I can see it in the swell of his chest, his pumped-up reaction as I feed his ego. I don't mind doing it—not when I'm stating facts.

He runs his forefinger along his lower lip and rubs at his chin. 'You've done your homework.'

'Of course.'

I don't want to say I knew all this anyway. That he might have been out of my life but I couldn't help keeping tabs on him. It's not like anyone can ignore him anyway, not when he's splashed all over the media to enjoy.

'I thought you said you needed time to prep for our meeting?' he says.

My cheeks colour. He's got me, and I look at my mug to avoid his eye, taking a sip. 'I like to know who I'm meeting. If I'm expecting Houston Logistics, I want to see Houston Logistics.'

'Are you saying you prefer dear old Leslie's company to mine?'

'I think from a distribution point of view you're on a par.'

'You know that's not what I meant.'

'Isn't it?' I challenge—and, God help me, my belly flutters excitedly. Sparring with him is too much fun.

He gives a soft laugh. 'Fair enough, but I disagree. We're not on a par. Open your email. I've sent you some comparisons to look at it.'

'Comparisons?' I place my coffee on the desk and look at my computer screen, doing as he asks.

'Sure. I figured I'd make it easy for you. In the attachments you'll find a whole host of competitors and the reason Waring Holdings outperforms them all.'

I open up his email and the first attachment, giving it a quick scan, and then the next, and the next.

What the hell?

'How can you—?'

'How can I know who I'm up against? Your launch party told me that, and my research team did the rest. I may be missing a few—in fact I'm sure I will be—but if they're not on my radar they're not worth worrying about.'

I can't believe it. A thorough analysis worthy of myself or my team is laid out before me. It wouldn't take me long to check what the reports say for accuracy, but I know in my gut that I won't find anything to fault.

And then Nate's words come back to haunt me—his

timely text from Friday night, the multitude of commu-nications since: *You can't trust him.*

I look at Lucas now and Nate's warning clashes with what I know for myself, with what I feel.

Why did he want me to see that Nate had called? Was it his way of saying his conscience is clear? That he's not worried about him or what he has to say? And if his conscience is clear, then what does that say about my brother? My family?

A wave of uncertainty washes over me and I throw my focus into the spreadsheets and the words before me. But they simply blur.

Lucas left, though. The company collapsed, my brother and father dealt with the fallout, and Lucas was long gone. Why didn't he stick around and protest his innocence? At least help? Why did he go without say-ing goodbye?

And there it is—the crux of it.

Christ, it was hardly like you spent any time together by then. He owed you nothing.

But the pain is there, and I know it's a huge part of it all. He left without so much as a nod in my direc-tion, without even attempting to clear his name with me, and he must have known the crap my family would lay at his feet.

'What really happened?' I say, looking at the screen.

'Excuse me?'

I look at him now, my eyes narrowed. 'Between you and Nate…the company?'

He stills, his posture straight as his eyes fall away from me. 'You should talk to *him* about it.'

'I'm talking to you.'

Not to mention that it's the last thing I want to raise with Nate. He went off the rails for two years after the company collapsed, drinking heavily, socialising day and night—he was a mess. No one talks about it. Least of all me.

'If we're potentially going to work together, I want to hear your version of events.'

'It's not my place.'

'The hell it's not! You left when the going got tough—is that how it was? Because that's exactly how my family see it. Things got a touch hard and you legged it, leaving them to pick up the pieces.'

Colour seeps into his cheekbones, his knuckles whiten around the mug he still holds, and his eyes harden as they land on me.

'You don't know what you're talking about.'

'Then tell me—give me your side and I'll consider you as equally as I am everyone else.'

'My company stands for itself. I'm not justifying the past to you.'

'You told me Friday night that you make it your business to know all there is about the companies you wish to work with and the people who run them. This is me doing the same due diligence.'

He leans forward in his chair and I think he is about to speak. I hold my breath, waiting. This is it: the truth, his side to balance out theirs.

'Thank Clare for the coffee.'

What?

He places his mug on the desk and gets to his feet. I stand abruptly. 'You can't leave.'

'Changed your mind already?'

There's humour in his words but not in his eyes.

'We have things to discuss, to go over,' I say.

'It's all there in the email. The last attachment details the arrangement I propose. I think you'll find it fair.'

'But—'

'Speak to Nate, Eva, or drop the past.'

His tone brooks no argument, but how can I tell him I don't dare have it out with my brother for fear of a relapse?

'My business references speak for themselves. Speak to anyone about Waring Holdings and they will put your mind at ease…if it's truly the business you're worried about.'

He lifts his jacket from the back of the chair and shrugs it on, taking up his laptop and case.

'My number is in the email—call me when you're ready to talk business.'

And with that he leaves. I haven't even managed a goodbye. I'm still floundering under the mess that is the past and the present, my family and my business—and, if I'm truly honest, my heart.

To think I had believed it possible to be around him again and keep it tucked away was ridiculous.

Maybe in some way I hoped the past would protect me, keep me safe from falling again. And maybe it would have, if not for the fact that the past as I know it—as my family know it—could well be based on a lie. Or a clever manipulation of the truth. My brother was a pro at doing both when he wanted to.

And Lucas's words in my kitchen about his ten-year wait... They told me there was more to his rejection than I believed all those years ago.

But where does any of that leave me now?

If the company failure was down to Nate, why would Lucas want to go into business with another Beaumont? Why would he sleep with me?

I don't want to think of it as some sort of vendetta, but I can't help it. The rejected eighteen-year-old still inside me can't believe his sudden turnaround. *Get in business with the little sister...get in bed with her.*

It makes for the greatest revenge. But...

'I've had ten years to wait for this.'

Surely that shows he cares about me? Not my family, not my business, but *me*?

I want answers. To explain ten years ago, five years ago. I want the whole damn lot.

And that means going after him.

My phone starts to buzz, along with my watch, and I know it's Nate again without even looking. I ignore it.

I'm going to finish going through the email. I'm going to get my meetings done for the day. And then I'm going get my head around all of this.

If only it can be as simple as it sounds.

CHAPTER SIX

I POUND THE paving beneath my feet, trying to run her out of my system, to forget her family and the past. Tower Bridge and its array of lights against the night sky make the perfect scene to lose myself and regain peace. And normally it works. But not today.

I've had five years to bury the anger the Beaumonts spark in me, the resentment, the betrayal, but it's still as raw as if it was yesterday.

I've done this to myself. I should have stayed away.

There are other products, other investment opportunities—plenty to occupy me. The truth is, when you have money it's easy to make money—so long as you're careful. Nate should have remembered that five years ago, instead of taking it upon himself to sign a deal that I'd already warned him against.

No, not warned. *Forbidden.* Yet he'd broken my trust and done it anyway.

And, hey, presto: today's mess.

Although I can't really blame him for what's happening right now. For *her.* Life was fine. I wasn't fulfilled, but I was a damn sight happier than this.

Yes, it would have been easy enough for me to find opportunities elsewhere, but did I? No. I went knocking on her door, telling myself it was for the product.

The reality hits me—winds me, even—and I double over, my fingers gripping my thighs as I stare unseeingly at the ground.

I went for *her*.

It's obvious now. So obvious I can't believe I didn't see it in the first place. I told myself it was the instant hit of mutual attraction at the party that blurred the boundaries, but like hell it was.

Idiot. I smack my knees in frustration and take off at a sprint, uncaring that people are looking at me as if I'm crazy.

I *am* crazy.

Crazy to have reopened this old wound, brought back the past, her, Nate, the family I once belonged to, was loyal to.

I always cited that loyalty as the reason I stopped myself from giving in to the feelings I had for her. Now that loyalty is gone it's bloody obvious it was an excuse, a handy barrier to stop myself getting too close to someone else.

If my own mother wasn't able to love me, and my father was never in the picture, how could I expect someone else to? Someone who didn't *have* to? That kind of unconditional love doesn't exist. Eva's family proved that to me when they booted me out to protect Nate's arse. Now no one gets that close to me—no one has that kind of power over me.

No one but her, it seems. *Fuck*.

I round the corner to my building. I have an apartment above the company headquarters, which makes life easy when I'm working late. It's time to hit the shower and go out. Maybe a few drinks and a female companion will fit the bill.

Even my cock mocks me. No one will make me forget her—not now. Everything we've shared, every intense second has only ramped up the way I feel. It's like an obsession, an addiction, and neither is healthy or acceptable but I am powerless to stop it.

And as if to prove my point I see her—in the foyer of my building, chatting to security. She's leaning on their high-rise desk, legs crossed at the ankles. Judging by the sin-inspiring shoes, she hasn't changed since I saw her at work, only donned the black coat that's tied tight at the waist.

I stop short, staring through the glass as though at any moment she will vanish. And then I hear her laugh. It escapes through the door as someone opens it to leave and there's no mistaking it.

I realise belatedly that the person is holding the door open for me, and I give him a brief nod of thanks as I take hold of it.

But I don't enter—not yet.

I'm wrapped up in watching her, so relaxed, at ease, chatting, and the way others respond to her, get caught up in her happy web. Just like at the party, where everyone hung on her every word. Now she has Ron—a security guard, built like a wrestler, with a face that doesn't smile—beaming like a man-child.

And then he spies me, clears his throat as he gives a brief nod.

She steps back, turns to face me.

I move before her eyes reach me, striding into the foyer. 'I wasn't expecting to see you again so soon.'

I scan her face as I get nearer, looking for any hint as to what's brought her here.

Has she spoken to Nate? Does she know the truth? Is she here to discuss it? Or the deal?

All these questions blaze through my mind, racing with the crazy heat her nearness instils, but I can read nothing other than surprise in her face, in the flare to her eyes and her parted lips.

Which is odd since it's *my* building—who else does she expect to see?

And then heat flushes up her chest, her mouth snaps shut, her eyes drop and she fiddles with the handbag over her shoulder. 'I thought we could talk...'

She wets her lips nervously and looks up into my face. She's all demure and inviting at once, and I can only just about manage, 'Now?'

'If you're free...'

If I wasn't, I know I'd be making myself so. 'Have you eaten?' I ask.

I don't know why I'm proposing dinner, but I haven't eaten, and I suspect she hasn't found time to either. And dinner feels *safe*.

Safer than the other thing that springs to mind.

My body throbs with it. Sex with Eva. I want her so much it hurts. There's the ache of longing, of desire, but there's a greater ache—a riskier one, the one I know I should listen to. Dinner in a public place will help.

'Erm…no.'

'Let's talk over dinner. I just need a quick shower.'

The mention of a shower has her cheeks flushing deeper. 'Shall I wait here?' she asks.

My sanity says *yes*. Having her in my place would be too intimate. It would be too easy. And the look in her eyes is feeding that realisation.

'Don't be ridiculous. Come up and I'll fix you a drink.'

She looks to the security guard as I move off. 'Thanks, Ron.'

And then she falls into step beside me as I head to the lift, the doors already opening to greet us.

Every one of my senses, pumped up from my run, is doing overtime as we enter the space together and that warning ache builds. I use my pass to send the lift to my private floor and step back—a feeble attempt at creating distance.

'Nice run?'

I murmur an incoherent 'yes' and keep my eyes fixed ahead. It's hard enough that her perfume fills the space. To look at her in this private enclosure will tip me over. Make me think to hell with security cameras and giving Ron an eyeful.

'Something wrong?'

She's looking at me. I can make out her confused

'I've had ten years to wait for this.'

It's as if some kind of screen has lifted—as if I can see him clearly now and see him clearly then. So much emotion in his face. Did he feel something deeper for me all those years ago…something akin to what I felt… is he feeling it now?

I can see the fight in him. He won't speak. And suddenly I don't need words. I need *him*. *All* of him.

'Lucas…' I whisper, my lashes already lowering and my body lifting onto my toes as my head tilts back to find his mouth.

His body turns rigid, but he doesn't push me away. I kiss the corner of his mouth, its hard line, his five o'clock shadow grazing me. His scent is musky and all man, and I'm high on it. Every sensation teases me, even the slightest press of my lips against him.

He stays rock solid, unmoving, but I press on. I'm ready. For this…for whatever is to come. It feels right— *he* feels right.

I keep my eyes hooked on his, my hand upon his cheek as I reach for his beer bottle, taking it from his unresisting fingers and placing it on the table at my hip. Nerves rear up inside me, mixing with the thrum of anticipation, but I *want* this. And I think—*I know*— he wants it too.

I lift myself towards him again and gently nudge his mouth with my own. So hard, unrelenting. But I persist, taking what I've always wanted. Repeating the move, slow and coaxing. He tastes of beer, of him…

'Evangeline… *Don't*…'

He sounds gruff, pained, and I look into his eyes, see need shining back at me shrouded in fear.

'Don't what, Lucas? Press you for answers…?' My lips brush against his as I speak. 'Or do this?'

I tease the joining of his mouth with my tongue and his lashes flutter closed, his body shuddering on a stilted breath. And then he comes alive. His eyes open and there's no hesitation, no fear, just the burning heat of desire as he forks his fingers in my hair and swings me back against the wall.

The first sweep of his tongue against mine turns my body molten, and the explosive heat swirling in the pit of my stomach is mounting the further he invades, the harder he moves over me. Hungry, fierce, possessive.

I match him move for move, telling him with my body what I want, what I need. No games, no taking control. This is about *us*. I feel as if I'm drowning in a multitude of emotions and sensations and I can't cling to a single one. I'm hungry for them all.

'If we let this go on I won't stop,' he says, intense.

I drag him back to me, press my body into his hardness. 'I don't want you to stop—not ever.'

Christ, that's a sweeping statement, but I'm done holding back. I'm living for this moment.

He breaks away from me completely and I look at him, pleading. *Please… Don't stop…not now…*

His eyes blaze at me and his jaw pulses with such tension. I know he wants me. I *know* it. I can feel it, for Christ's sake.

Before panic truly sets in, he grasps my hand and

starts to stride away. I don't know where we're going and I don't care. As long as we're together…as long as we complete this.

The foyer is vast, with several doors, and he pushes open the double doors that sit at the end.

The master suite. *His* master suite.

It's masculine, stark, moody—so *him*.

He releases my hand but is still walking as he drags his sports tee over his head. I am rooted, just watching him—every muscle that ripples, the trace of sweat, the strength of his arousal as he turns to me and kicks off his shoes, his socks, his shorts, his boxers—

Oh, God.

Heat assaults my gut. Sheer, intense heat.

'You owe me a shower,' he grinds out.

My mouth is so dry I don't think I can speak. Instead I lift my fingers to my blouse in answer and begin unbuttoning it. All the while I watch him. Watch how he follows my fingers and his cock lifts. A whimper sounds in my throat. I can't contain it. I feel as if I'll burst if I don't have him soon.

He draws in a breath, flexing his fists at his sides, and then he's across the room before I know it, his hands on my blouse, parting it, thrusting it down my body. The force of the move spikes my libido, making my tummy contract with the rush.

'Too slow,' he complains, yanking it free of my wrists and tugging me against him so hard I gasp.

The heat of his body sears my bare skin, my breasts surge within my bra and his impressive arousal presses between us, making the dull ache down low a pulsing knot.

He reclaims my mouth, his tongue plundering, taking my all.

'I can't believe you kept this from me.'

He says it between kisses, as if at any moment I might pull away, and I know he's referring to my *No Kissing* rule.

'You feel incredible. You *taste* incredible.'

He sounds like a man half-starved, and I cling to him as he reaches down my back, his fingers grazing over my tingling skin to unzip my skirt. He forces it down my hips, letting gravity do the rest as he drops his hands to cup my arse, drawing me harder against him.

He pulses between us, a growl erupting low in his throat, and I raise my leg to hook it around him, encouraging him closer, bringing his rigid length right up against my clit. Pleasure ripples through me, and his mouth swallows my moan as he keeps on kissing me.

And I'm kissing him back. Intense, possessive. As if we're branding one another with our claim.

He drops his hand to cup my thigh and goes still, his forehead pressing into mine as he twists his head to look at where his hand is on me over the lace band of my hold-ups.

'*Fuck*, Evangeline… You're too sexy.'

I laugh, almost delirious at hearing those words come from his lips. I'm dreaming, surely. But his hardness, his heat, his breath as it sweeps over my chest in ragged gusts is all real. Erotic, carnal and *happening*.

He grabs my other leg and hauls me up against him, wrapping them around his waist. Then he's moving, his mouth back on mine and his eyes on the direction in which we're travelling. He strides across the room into the adjacent bathroom and presses me up against the cold tiles. My body shivers at the chill even as I worship the sensation: the cold at my back, his heat at my front…

He reaches out to mess with a dial.

Water pounds the marble floor, the sound blending with the rush of blood in my ears and the moans of sheer abandon that I'm barely aware of making. I hold his face in my hands. Gripping him to me. My mouth, my tongue are unable to get enough of this. And then he sets me down and tears his lips away to trace a searing path along my jaw, down my throat.

I lean back against the wall, my body trembling with need as I arch into him, encouraging him lower, *needing* him lower, running my hands over his shoulders, down his back.

He undoes the clasp of my bra and my breasts bloom, heat rushing to their tips as he eases the cups aside and the straps down. It falls to our feet as his hands roughly cup me, his mouth claiming one pleading bud, moving tantalisingly over it, his tongue flicking before drawing it in deep.

Christ.

I claw at his shoulders, my desire mounting, out of control. 'I *need* you.'

He takes in the other nipple, his hands turning more

urgent, his mouth unrelenting. We move against one another, our bodies building into a crazed rhythm.

I reach for him, desperate to feel him, to ride him. My fingers close around his cock, its heat feeding into my palm as I draw my hand upwards. He hisses, throwing his head back, and I repeat the move, watching his efforts to fend off his climax so clearly building.

And then he grabs at my wrist, pulling away. *'Not again,'* he bites out, his fingers rough as he yanks my thong down.

I step out of it and he turns to my high heels, stripping them off so swiftly I'm sent off balance. But his palm is there, on my torso, pinning me against the wall as he drops to his knees. The heat of his touch contends with the intense heat swelling out of control just beneath, and then his mouth is there, at the heart of it all, his tongue sweeping over my clit and making me buck, making me cry.

His fingers smooth around my thighs, slipping beneath the tops of my hold-ups. He rolls them down, and all the while his tongue is circling my clit, gently goading me, driving me crazy.

He lifts one foot to pull the nylon free, then the other, but he doesn't stand. He's too busy feasting off me, his hands coming up to part me, to give his mouth, his tongue, deeper access, and I know I'm going to come. I can feel it building in my limbs.

But I want him inside me. I want all of him when I do.

I pull at him, my nails running up his shoulders. 'No, not like this.'

His voice rumbles over me. He doesn't agree.

'Lucas.'

Something in my voice makes him pause and he leans back on his haunches, looking up at me. I'm wondering why the hell I stopped him, but...

'I need you inside me.'

The pulse works in his jaw and then he's on his feet, striding away.

What the fuck?

He's back in seconds, sheathing himself, and the sight of his fingers moving masterfully over his erection is so fucking erotic, even as I acknowledge that he's had the sense to get protection when I didn't.

I start backing into the shower, pulling the pins from my hair, undoing my hair tie, dropping them to the floor. All the while my eyes are fixed on his, taunting him to come and get me.

Water rushes over my body and I tilt my head back, lifting my fingers to comb through my hair. And then his own are upon mine, completing the move. His lips claim me, hard and demanding. Water runs between us, slips into our mouths, our eyes. His cock presses against my stomach, stoking the fierce ache within.

'Please, *now*,' I beg.

He runs his hands down my body in answer, cupping my thighs to lift me against him.

I encircle his waist and he takes himself in his hand between us, positioning himself, positioning me. His look of concentration damn near pushes me over. And then he's there, his tip nudging at my entrance, and I clamp down on my lower lip as I take his sweet invasion. He's slow, measured, his restraint taking all his effort, and I know he doesn't want to hurt me. He wants it to be right.

I move over him, coaxing him further, deeper, stretching to take him. More. *More.* Until he fills me completely and I moan, contracting around him even as he stills, his breath hissing between his teeth. He's trembling, fighting for control. But I don't want his control. I want his total abandon.

I nip his lower lip with my teeth, drawing his mouth back to me, pushing his concentration away, and I undulate over him, slowly at first, using my every yoga-toned muscle to guide him, tease him.

And then he's moving, taking the driving seat. He forces me back against the wall, his rigid length riding my clit from within as he pumps harder, faster. Our teeth clash, our tongues twist, our kiss as erotic as the action below.

Yes. Yes. Yes.

Pleasure radiates from my toes up and the muscles of my legs tighten as it builds. I can't move now. He drives it all as ecstasy renders my body immobile and then it erupts, shaking through my entire body as I cry out. He thrusts deeper, his own cry drowning out my own, and he loses it with me.

It's so perfect, so utterly right. But even as I come down from the crest of the wave, my legs still hooked around him, now limp with release, I know that's a fanciful notion.

Because whatever his words mean, whatever his keeping the photo means, whatever the cause of his fall-out with Nate, it doesn't change the fact that my family won't accept him. They won't accept *this*. I doubt even Lucas will accept it when all is said and done.

And if that's the case, what the hell am I doing fanta-sising about the impossible? Teasing myself with *what if...?*

He brushes his lips against my neck, his caress soft and barely there, and my thoughts fragment, disperse as sensation takes over...

'I could get lost in you, Evangeline.'

CHAPTER SEVEN

I FEEL HER tense around me.

Fuck.

I curse my mammoth mouth.

What the hell is wrong with me? I don't *ever* speak without thinking first. Yet she's done this to me, with the turnaround in her no kissing rule and what it means to her, to me. There's no way in hell I would usually say anything as sentimental, as deep as that—not if I'd taken the time to think first.

It was impulsive, reckless.

There can be no getting lost for me in *anyone*. Especially her. A Beaumont. The one woman with the power to crucify me, to rip my heart out and leave me stranded. Lost. I've been that person. I won't be like that again.

'What did you say?'

She encourages my head up and I shut my expression down with a grin. 'Nothing.'

She's frowning at me and I spin her into the water flow. It's noisy in here—noisy enough for her to doubt she heard me right. I cling to that, setting her down on her feet.

'Let me get rid of this... Stay here.'

I stride out of the shower, avoiding my reflection in the mirrors that run along one wall as if my reflection will only incriminate me further. There's a bin in the bathroom but I don't use it. I keep going until I'm in my bedroom and I can take a steadying breath out of sight, take a few seconds to gather my wits before I face her again.

Lost...

It wasn't a lie.

My lungs contract, my chest aches. I strip off the condom and toss it in the wastebin beside the dressing table. My reflection in the mirror above it catches me, and I see the torrent of emotion in my face.

But it's just sex. It has to be.

Sex now. Work later. The end.

I'd laugh if it wasn't so brutal. So impossible to think of bringing an end to this thing between us.

She appears in the entrance to my bathroom, a towel wrapped around her, her brows drawn together, and I shut everything down under the wave of warmth the sight inspires.

'I said stay there.' I stride towards her, swinging her up into my arms.

She laughs in surprise, her hands hooking around my neck. 'I thought you'd run out on me.'

I look into her face, my grin purposefully easy. 'Would I do that?'

There's a moment's hesitation in her face and then I'm kissing her, pushing out everything else as I walk straight back into the shower, uncaring of the towel still wrapped around her.

'Lucas…' She pants as she presses me away, her eyes dancing. 'The towel…'

I look down at it. 'Ah, well, too late now.'

I set her down and strip it from her, tossing it aside as I flick my wet hair from my eyes and take her in my arms. Her flushed skin is wet, and marked where I've been, and a primal surge of possessiveness assaults me, winds me.

Her eyes flicker beneath the droplets of water, as if she's read it all, and she lifts her palm to my chest. 'Keep looking at me like that and I'll think it's *me* you're wanting for dinner.'

I comb her hair back from her face, the water with it. 'How about actual food for dinner and you for dessert?'

Her smile is soft, and she lowers her eyes—to avoid the run of the water or to hide, I'm not sure. And I do the one thing I know to bring her back to me and get the answer I want. I kiss her. Slow and teasingly. Until she's kissing me back and her hands are holding tight.

Then I break away. 'Deal?'

'Deal…' she breathes.

I draw her tight against me, feeling her approval upping the rush of my desire. I know I have to let the real world back in soon, but for now it can stay the hell away.

Reality comes sooner than I expect or want—in the shape of her blasted smartwatch again. I want to rip it from her. Insist she put it away, and her phone with it.

We're sitting on my living room floor, not too far from recreating a scene from our teens, with Chinese takeaway boxes strewn across my coffee table. She's in one of my T-shirts, her hair loosely piled atop her head, her face clean and glowing from our hot shower and the multitude of heated acts since. I'm on one side of the table and she is on the other, stretched out and perfect.

Save for that damn watch.

She looks at it and that frown is back.

'I assume it's your watch and not the food doing that?'

'Hmm...?' She looks at me, distracted, and I lean over to touch her brow, smoothing it.

'The frown?'

She gives me a look which I interpret as an apology and wraps her legs beneath her as she takes up a spring roll. She's forcing a calmness she doesn't feel—I know it. But I'm silent, pressing.

She takes a bite and the food breaks into her mouth, vegetable strands escaping as she licks them up. Her dainty tongue is efficient and far more sexual than it has any right to be. She's doing it on purpose—trying to distract me, I'm sure.

But there's also unease building, and I want it gone.

She makes a delectable little hum in her throat. 'No, the food is fantastic.'

I barely hear the words I'm so focused on the satisfying sound and on her lips as they turn the food over.

Distracted?

I force my focus. 'So, what is it?'

Silently she chews, her eyes on me as if she's gauging my potential reaction.

'I'm not about to kick you out in just my T-shirt if that's what you're worried about—you can tell me.'

Her lips quirk. 'No, I don't think you'd do that.'

'Then tell me.'

She looks me over and that unease mounts.

'It's nothing, I'm just...' She shrugs. 'I'm just enjoying this. It's nice...like old times.'

'I've been thinking the same.'

I like that she feels it too. *Really* like it. And it's a problem—I know it is—but the warmth it brings is there regardless.

Suddenly she gives a little giggle and that cosy feeling inside me blooms, edging out the unease. 'What?' I ask.

'You remember that time when Mum went all vegetarian on our arses and wouldn't let a scrap of meat into the house?'

My smile is instant, the memory as vivid as yesterday. 'You mean the ribs fiasco?'

She giggles again and I hook on to the sound. It's so carefree, so easy. 'I don't think that Chinese takeaway had any left by the time you, Nate and I finished raiding it.'

'True—but Nate was the worst offender. He could put away a truckload.'

'Yeah, but it was *your* idea.' She looks at me and licks her lips. 'You were mortified when Mum found the remains in the bin the next day.'

'Can you blame me? If you'd only taken the bin out, like you were supposed to, that never would have happened.'

'Well, you and Nate got your own back—tossing me into the pool fully clothed.'

A wicked rush surges south and I tense against it. I remember that moment too. And I remember when she stepped out of the pool, soaked and ranting, not realising that her white tee clung to her every curve. It was a month before her eighteenth birthday, and the day I acknowledged that my feelings towards her had changed.

Unfortunately Nate had sensed it too.

I clear my throat and shake my head at her. 'You deserved it.'

'Hmph…' she says over her spring roll, her eyes alive and holding my own.

I don't want this to end.

'Stay the night?' It's out before I can stop it, but I manage to avoid adding *please*, begging.

Her lashes lower; her eyes flicker away.

The mood is shattered—once again thanks to my big mouth.

She drops the last bite of spring roll onto her plate and wipes her fingers on some kitchen towel. 'I can't.'

'Why?'

It's more abrupt than I want to be, but I know that after she leaves we won't get this back—this moment, this connection.

Her watch goes off again, her phone echoing the buzz, and she glances at it.

Anger fires in my veins. I know the answer even before I ask, 'Who is it, Eva?'

Her eyes flick to mine, her cheeks now pale. 'I think
you know.'

'Your father…mother…Nate…?'

'Try all of the above.'

She suddenly sounds tired, weary, and my body pulls
with the need to comfort her. Which is madness, since
I'm likely at the heart of it all. But I'm pissed off. I'm
sick of being seen as the bad guy. I loved every last one
of them and they…they…

Fuck, what does it matter?

'What's so urgent that they have to bombard you at
this time of night?' I can't keep the bitterness out of
my voice.

She gives an incredulous laugh, surprising me. 'You
can't guess?'

I take up my beer, having a slug before answering.
'Are they worried the evil Lucas Waring is leading you
astray?'

'Don't say that.'

'Why? It's the truth, isn't it?'

'They're just worried about me.'

'Good for them.'

'Lucas, please—if you just tell me what happened
then maybe I can help…maybe we can see a way to put
the past to bed.'

My laugh is derisive. 'You really don't know your
brother if that's what you think.'

Hell, I thought I knew him and look where it got me.

'You'd be surprised.'

There's something in the way she says it that has my ears pricking, my attention shifting. 'What's that supposed to mean?'

'Things changed after you left—*he* changed, and not for the better... He's...suffering.'

The admission is weighted, and she looks away from me as if she's said too much. I don't know whether to push or let it go. I should let it go. Digging further implies I care too much. About her, about Nate, her family. But I can't.

I lean back into the sofa behind me and take another swig of beer. 'Why don't you be straight with me and I'll be straight with you?'

He looks so relaxed in his stonewashed jeans and white tee, leaning back against his deep grey sofa, beer in hand. But it's his eyes that tell me otherwise. There's a dangerous glint to them that tells me to shut up. Even though I know we need to do this, get it all out in the open.

'Why don't you be straight with me and I'll be straight with you?'

It's what I came for.

And maybe if he understands the way things are with Nate now, he'll understand why I have no desire to interrogate my brother. Why I need to hear it from him.

I look at my near-empty bottle of beer. 'Can I get another?'

'You stalling?'

'Call it Dutch courage.'

I remember the last time I used that kind of courage to do what I needed to with him and my cheeks colour as I roll my shoulders, shaking it off. The move draws his eye and I tug at his T-shirt, feeling suddenly naked against his fully clothed state.

'You're sure you're ready to hear the lurid details of what happened five years ago? Sure you want your golden-boy brother tainted?'

Golden-boy? I almost snort and he sharpens his gaze. He doesn't miss a trick.

'About that beer…?' I say.

'About Nate…?'

I take a breath and raise my chin. 'I'll tell you exactly what the last five years have been like if you promise to tell me what happened.'

His eyes flicker; his jaw pulses. 'I've already agreed, and I don't go back on my word—no matter what *your* family think.'

The way he stresses 'your' isn't lost on me, and he slaps his beer bottle on the coffee table as he rises.

'But also know I still want dessert.'

My insides clench and my lips part. I'm so glad he isn't looking at me to see the effect his words have had. It doesn't matter how deep our conversation goes, how much pain it dredges up, his effect on me is impossible to prevent, and I need to muster my strength if I am to get through this unscathed.

Perhaps walking out, ringing Nate, dealing with his ineffectual tantrum, would be preferable to opening myself up even more to Lucas. I was vulnerable enough before, but now...

I don't finish the thought. Instead I scoop up the empty trays and roll the leftovers onto one plate. My mind shifts helplessly to 'dessert'.

What the fuck, Eva?

I know I shouldn't be contemplating it. Loyalty is a huge thing in my family—we stand by one another through thick and thin. The Beaumonts stand united, as Dad would say. But everything I've done with Lucas, everything I *am* doing, goes against that.

Or does it?

I'm only trying to get to the truth, to get the other side to this tale.

I join him in the kitchen. 'Where's your bin?'

I scan his super-smooth cupboards, the walls—avoid looking at the solitary framed photo.

'Here.' He presses a rectangle and out it pops. I drop the rubbish in as he turns to me with a beer bottle.

'Ta.'

My hand rests over his as I take it. Our eyes lock and the crazy narration taking place in my brain ceases and then starts again tenfold.

Why does he have this power? No one else has ever come close. No one...

'Evangeline.'

His voice rasps and suddenly it annoys me. I'm sick of being out of control with him. Sick of being hounded by my family to do *the right thing*.

'Let's talk.'

I stride back to the living area and sink onto the sofa, my legs curled up alongside me.

He's slower than me to return. 'Is it safe to sit next to you?'

'If you like.'

I don't look at him as he lowers himself onto the sofa. I focus on chucking back a mouthful of beer rather than on the way my body reacts to his proximity, the fuzzy warmth that radiates all down the side that's closest to him. I taste nothing.

'So?' he probes, looking at me.

But I don't turn. Reliving the past isn't something I find easy. It changed me for the better, made me stronger, more determined to go after what I want and gain my independence. Nate's the opposite.

'Nate's not the man you remember.'

'So you say.'

I give him a quick look, more to shut him up than anything. His cold dismissal isn't what I need right now.

'It wasn't like it happened overnight,' I say. 'At first it just seemed like he was putting in enough hours for two, filling in for his AWOL partner—'

'I wasn't—'

I cut him off with another look. 'You want me to tell you how things went down over here when you swanned off to the States or not?'

'Apologies—go on…' He retreats, his shoulders relaxing as he sinks back into the sofa and gestures with the tail end of his bottle as he drinks.

I tear my gaze from the movement in his throat as he

swallows and look at my bottle, toying with the corner of its label as I work out where to start.

'He started to become hard to reach,' I say eventually. 'We'd have people messaging us to say they'd seen him in this bar, this club, this restaurant, asking if he was okay. Which was bizarre in itself. I mean, Christ, he was a grown adult, but even I, his younger sister, was getting concerned messages.'

Hair falls over my eyes as the memory makes me animated. I scrape it behind my ear and throw back some beer, letting it settle before I carry on.

'We put it down to him networking at first—trying to pull in investors to save the company. But of course that was a load of rubbish. The company was past saving. The highlight came when he got himself into a fight. I mean, I knew he was quick to temper—how could I not, being his annoying little sister? But losing it with a sibling is very different to a public fist fight with a billionaire you're trying to impress.'

Lucas clears his throat and I sense he knows this already—the incident made it into the papers so it's no surprise.

'Dad insisted he come home for a bit. He helped him get straightened out, gave him a role in the family business and what-have-you, but he was never the same... not without you.'

I expect Lucas to say something, but he doesn't, so I press on.

'He doesn't trust himself. Dad thinks he's okay now but he's not. He calls me too often, asking my opinion, needing advice on things that he really shouldn't need me for. And then when things go south it's me that gets the call.'

'Christ, Eva, you have your own work—you shouldn't be wiping his arse.'

I see red. Hot tears burn my throat as my eyes snap to his. 'Maybe if you'd stuck around longer it never would have come to this. He missed you—needed you.'

He pales, and I wonder who I'm really talking about. Me or Nate.

Does it really matter when the same applies?

I look at the bottle in my hand, stare through it. 'Maybe if you'd actually bothered to pick up your phone and help, you could have changed things.'

Bad enough that he'd upped and left, but then he'd ignored my phone calls, my pleas for help…

It didn't matter that we had nothing much to do with one another any more. That avoidance was my way of coping after the lesson of my eighteenth birthday. But I still thought I deserved something—he owed us, owed *me*.

'I called you almost daily at first, and I texted, emailed. Then one day your phone stopped working and my emails bounced. You were really gone.'

'I'm sorry.'

I glance at him. His hand is so tight around the beer bottle's neck I fear he's going to break it.

'What for?' I demand. 'Ignoring me? Or what you did to Nate?'

'I had to cut myself off.'

'*Had* to or wanted to?'

He shakes his head. 'It was a choice that was made for me.'

I scoff. 'No one tells you what to do, Lucas. You've always done what you want, when you want.'

'If that was the case I wouldn't have stopped myself at your eighteenth.'

His voice is harsh, formidable, the truth in his words undeniable. I don't know what I expected but it wasn't that. I can't find any words—can't seem to make a sound.

'That really surprises you so much?'

'Lucas, I…'

This isn't getting the right answers—this is getting into *us*, and 'us' isn't going to help me get my family straightened out, end their feud and bring me the decision I need to make for my business.

'I wanted you, Evangeline. I wanted to drag you off to a quiet corner, ride that dress up your hips and take all that you were offering me.'

My heart rises in my throat. I can't breathe past the desire and the bigger emotion that's holding my lungs tight. 'Then why…?'

It's a whisper so quiet I can barely hear it above the racing pulse in my ears.

'I told you that night—because of *Nate*.'

He says it so fiercely, his body rigid as he considers me.

'He told me to keep away… What? You didn't believe me?'

'No. Yes.' I shake my head. I can't believe Lucas would give up on us because my brother had ordered it so. 'I don't know.'

'He left me in no doubt as to what would happen if I went there with you.'

I flip. The pain I suffered, my heart ripped in two. 'He was your best friend—not your keeper! *Christ*, you even went out with his exes and vice versa. Why was *I* so different?'

'You were out of bounds. You were his little sister.'

My scoff is more of a snort this time. But this is madness. I *won't* believe it.

'You can't blame him for wanting to protect you. My reputation with the opposite sex didn't exactly work in my favour.'

No, I remember his reputation well enough. It made it all the more painful when he rejected me—as if I didn't come up to scratch.

'Look, Eva, he was my best friend—the closest thing to family. You all were. Why is it so hard for you to believe I didn't want to jeopardise that?'

I can read the truth in the softening of his eyes. I want to scream that I should have been more important, that I wanted him, loved him, but it all seems so selfish now.

And ultimately it didn't matter. He lost it all anyway. Nate, their friendship, my family…

'Fat lot of good it did you.'

I neck my beer, washing down the bitter bite of my words.

'Believe me, I'm more than aware of what I gave up then.'

I ignore the flare to my heart his passion instils. His old feelings towards me don't help now. If I was out of bounds before, when my family loved him, I'm on another playing field now.

He reaches for me, his fingers brushing the hair behind my ear. 'Evangeline, I *am* sorry.'

I risk a look and butterflies flutter in my throat at what I see—his sincerity, his intensity. He's so close. I'd only have to lean a little to meet him, to kiss him. And I want to so much. To drown out the pain with the crazy passion that simmers just beneath the surface.

I know he's thinking the same—I can feel it in the touch of his fingers still stroking at my skin, see it in the parting of his lips, the darkening of his eyes.

'I really am sorry…'

He's closer—too close. I have a second to stop this, before it goes too far, and I almost don't. It would be too easy to forget it all in his kiss.

I suspect he knows it—that he's doing it on purpose—and it's that which has me pushing at his chest, straightening my body and forcing his hand to fall away.

I need answers. I need to know.

'It's your turn,' I say. 'What happened five years ago?'

CHAPTER EIGHT

HER EYES ARE fixed on mine. She's not going to let it go.

It wasn't as if I'd tried to kiss her to make her forget. *Honest.* Although it would have been preferable to this.

I place my beer on the table and rake my hands through my hair. I don't owe Nate anything. And yet talking about it doesn't come easy. Last time I spoke up I lost the entire family. Her father pushed me out and told me I'd failed them, failed Nate. He was angry, but his words stung. More than he can possibly know.

And how would she take it—*the same way?*

I meet her determined gaze and realise it doesn't matter how she reacts. She isn't going to let it rest until she knows. And I have nothing to be ashamed of.

Nothing.

Not that her father saw it that way.

'Well?' She tucks her legs tight beneath her, the challenge in her eyes bright. It beats tears. They knotted up my insides, crushed me with guilt.

I speak over the painful reminder. 'You know what your brother was like growing up: outgoing, a people-pleaser, a constant beam of optimism?'

She frowns at me, but nods. I know she's comparing how he was to the man he is now, as she's just described him to me.

'He was also hot-headed, excitable—he would always act first, think later, if it meant he could lead the way with whatever had caught his eye.'

I take up my beer for a swig and let the memories in.

'He definitely did that when it came to women.' I can almost laugh at that. 'We had some seriously fun times…and some fallouts. But it was the same in business too, and together we *worked*. So long as I was there, watching his back, and so long as he listened to me we were okay, the business was okay. He was the go-getter and I was the level-headed one, doing the research and giving final approval.'

'Yeah, I know. Dad made some sweeping comment not long after it all came crashing down, referring to you both as yin and yang, the perfect system…until you went AWOL.'

'I *didn't* go AWOL.' It comes through gritted teeth, and I see my anger surprises her. 'I left after your brother went too far with one of his schemes. He'd been pulled in by a woman he was dating. She'd convinced him this product they were working on was the next big thing—that they just needed enough investment and it would make us all billions.'

I laugh bitterly now, as I remember the conversation, the stupidity of it all.

'I told him it was a bad investment, that we couldn't risk it. We still had your father's money to pay back and

we were on track for that. A few months and we could
have been clear—well on our way to making a small for-
tune. Of course, your brother wasn't one for waiting, but
I never thought for a second he would go ahead and do
it without me. He lost it all. Bankrupted the company…
lost your father's money…left us with nothing.'

'But…' She's staring at me as if she doesn't believe
a word. 'I don't understand. Why did you leave if it
was all him?'

'I was angry. I tried to speak to your father but Nate
got there first—claimed I'd been on board, that he might
have sourced the deal but I was with him on it.'

'No, he wouldn't lie like that.'

She's shaking her head at me, but her voice is soft,
lacking in conviction. Not that I care whether she be-
lieves me or not. Her father didn't—why would she be
any different?

'Wouldn't he? Nate was always trying to prove himself, to outperform all around him, to prove his worth
to your father. Can you imagine what this did to him…?
No, you don't need to imagine—you *know*.'

'But to lie…to blame you.'

'I don't think he realised at the time just how badly
his accusation would land. He was just covering his
back, protecting his position with your father.'

'Fuck that, Lucas! You were kicked out because of
this.'

I don't need her sympathy or her anger. This is old
news to me.

'Your father chose to believe him. I tried to tell him

but he wouldn't listen. Ultimately I don't think he cared. He just wanted to place the blame squarely on me.' I take another swig of beer, douse the choking heat in my throat. 'I wasn't *blood*.'

'But, Lucas…' Her voice is whisper-soft. 'You could've come to *me*—at least told me, explained…'

'What good would that have done?'

'I could've spoken to Dad, defended you, made Nate come clean—anything.'

I shake my head at her. It doesn't change anything. The past is done and dusted. There can be no going back.

'I was better off out of it. I wasn't about to plough any more time and money into that company. I couldn't trust Nate any more—not in business and not personally either. He betrayed me, Eva. He was like my brother, and then he did something as huge as that behind my back and lied about it.'

'But what about *me*?'

'What about you?'

She chews her lip, eyes wide. 'Didn't I deserve to know?'

'You expected me to turn up and say, *Hey, Eva, not seen you since you were at your folks with your fiancé, all happy and whatnot, but get this: your brother just screwed me over and bankrupted the company, so I'm off. Sayonara*?'

The words come out rapidly and then it hits me. It wasn't just Nate and her father I ran from. It was her too. Her and her soon-to-be marriage.

Christ. I rake a shaky hand through my hair and evade her eyes.

'Don't be so ridiculous!'

I barely hear her. I'm reeling from the realisation that I am screwed. That coming back to her has opened me up, made me defenceless again. Vulnerable.

Her phone starts to ring, her watch vibrates. She flicks her wrist and cuts the call.

'Who was it?'

'Nate.'

The pain of the past, the potential future, has me snapping, 'Tell you what—why don't you leave so you can call him back?'

Her eyes widen. I can see I've hurt her but I can't hold back. I need to bury this crazed emotion boiling inside me.

'Don't push me away.'

'Your family did that a long time ago.'

'And I want to fix this.'

'You want the impossible.'

'No, I don't. Nate's not been the same since you left. It makes so much sense now why he doesn't trust himself— why he comes to me before Dad, why he's always looking for a sounding board. He needs you in his life again.'

Screw Nate. All I care about right now is *her*, and the dawning realisation that I ran from her all those years ago and I don't want to run any more.

'And you, Evangeline? Do *you* need me?'

'I—'

She breaks off as her phone rings again, and this

time she pushes to her feet and strides away, grabbing up her coat from the bar stool and taking her phone out of its pocket.

She lifts it to her ear. 'Just give me half an hour.'

Her eyes flick to mine as she listens to the person on the other end.

'I'm busy right now... Just busy... Out... Dinner... No, no one you know...'

'No one you know...'

I flex my hand around the beer bottle, keeping my face expressionless.

Her silence extends and she wets her lips. 'I get that... No, I know... Yes, I'll call you... Bye.'

She hangs up and pockets the phone, her eyes coming back to me, shadowed. 'Thank you for telling me the truth.'

'So I'm *no one you know*?' Anger at her lie heats my words, my body, my blood.

'What did you expect me to say?'

'I don't know.' I get to my feet. 'I'm not sure where I fall. Am I the guy you're fucking, or the guy you're going into business with?'

She swallows hard. 'Neither.'

My laugh is harsh. 'Well, your state of undress places me in the former camp, for sure.'

She tugs at the hem of my tee and her cheeks heat. 'We *were* fucking—now I have no idea what we're doing.'

'No? Want me to help with that?'

I walk towards her and she backs into the counter.

Perhaps a revenge fuck will kill off this insane sea of emotion. Something has to.

'No. I can't do this.' She raises her palm to me even as her nipples bead against the tee. Air rasps from her lungs. 'I need time to think about what you've said. It changes so much and yet changes nothing.'

I stop walking and my smile is tight. 'Okay, and while you're thinking it through can I take it that my business proposition meets with your approval?'

She starts moving towards my bedroom, her coat hooked over her arm. 'We need to talk about that.'

'Talk?'

I follow her. She's looking for her clothes, dipping and bending as she collects each item from its place on the floor. If not for the edge to her voice I'd be all over the sight of her bare arse each time my tee lifts.

'You say we need to talk like it's a way off?'

She dumps her clothing on the bed and with her back to me pulls my T-shirt over her head. My pulse leaps, heat streaks to my groin and I pocket my fists. She's not making this easy.

'I have concerns.'

She steps into her thong and shimmies it up her legs, her hips, over her perfect round arse. *Christ.*

'What kind of concerns?'

'Like how you can do it so cheap.' She dons her bra, the cups facing me momentarily before she tugs it around to the front and slips her arms in.

Effortless, easy...so sexy even in reverse.

'I care about my workforce, whether they work for

me or my suppliers. I need to know you're not crossing any human rights lines.'

She bends forward to step into her skirt but all I hear are the last three words. *'Human rights lines?* Who do you think I am?'

She looks at me over her shoulder as she fastens her skirt. 'Don't act so defensive. You wouldn't be the first company to present me with a proposal that takes advantage of child labour and suchlike.'

'Child labour...' I choke the words out—*is she kidding me?*

She's not looking at me now. She's thrusting her arms into her blouse and fastening it up, acting as if she has no awareness of how deep her words cut.

'Anyway, I don't want to discuss it now.'

She tucks her blouse into her skirt and strides into the bathroom, emerging with her shoes and stockings. She pushes her foot into one shoe and then the other, her eyes anywhere but on me.

'We can pick it up at work.'

She grabs up her coat and stuffs the delicate nylon strips into its pocket as she heads towards me, past me, back into the foyer, her eyes scanning the lift for a call button. I press it for her and she clears her throat.

'Thank you. My PA will be in touch to arrange a meeting.'

'Your PA?' I raise my brow at her, daring her to meet my eye. 'Why not you?'

'My PA and your PA can sort it out. It's the way of things, is it not?'

'Normally.'

She still won't look at me and it's driving me crazy. I want to reach for her and pull her in. I don't want her to go with this uncertainty hanging over us. I want to know where I stand.

And deep down I know it's not the business proposition I care about. It's her and her opinion of me. Is it so low that she could truly question my business ethics? I don't want to think it possible, and yet she's implying just that.

But then I never thought her father would think me a liar either...

And she's a Beaumont, after all.

The lift doors open and she sweeps inside, turning just quickly enough to offer me a parting look before they close.

And that look swallows me whole.

'What is it, Nate?'

My temper is frayed. I feel oddly naked with my stockings stuffed inside my coat pocket. As if every Londoner can tell I've just run out on my lover and didn't have the inclination to dress properly.

Your lover? Really, Eva.

'What do you mean: *what is it*?'

I tune in to my brother's scornful tone and take a breath before replying. It never pays to react in kind—especially with him.

'If this is about Lucas again, I'm not interested,' I say.

'If?'

I weave through the heavy stream of pedestrians, their loaded bags making it more awkward than usual. I really need to start my own Christmas shopping, but it's been at the back of mind, buried beneath work... *and now him.*

'What else would it be about?' asks Nate.

'I don't know—your issue with the wife of Mr Chan and her roaming fingers and the price hike they're insisting on? Or how about your laundry going astray?'

Okay, so I'm not doing a great job of keeping a lid on my frustration. I blame it on the ice-cold air whipping up my skirt and the thought of the heated body I'd much rather be curled up against and had to bail on to make this call.

No, not to make this call—to avoid getting in too deep.

Honesty was supposed to help. Instead it's opened me up...made me fall.

No. No. No. Not again.

'You're not funny, Eva.'

'Funny?' This really isn't what I call 'funny'. 'I wasn't trying to be.'

I look at the entrance to the Underground and decide against it. I can't face being hemmed in—not like this.

'Then quit the avoidance and tell me what you're playing at, still talking to him.'

I pause and a laden pedestrian curses, right on my tail.

'Sorry.' I grimace, ducking out of her way.

'Sorry?'

'Not you.' I scan the traffic, looking for a yellow taxi

light. 'I'm talking to him because he could be good for my business. He has everything I need.'

'*Need?*' Nate scoffs down the phone. 'There are plenty of other suitable firms. What about Rosalie and Janus Industries? She's flying in next week. I thought you were speaking to her?'

'I am.' I spy an available cab and hail it, moving to the edge of the kerb, careful to avoid being run down by either a person or a car. 'We're scheduled to meet on Tuesday.'

'So wait for her.'

I shake my head incredulously. 'Don't be ridiculous, Nate. I'm doing my research—both Rosalie's and Lucas's are among the many companies I'm considering. I'm getting this right.'

The cab pulls up alongside me and I open the door, hopping in. 'Jermyn Street, please.'

'Sure thing.'

The driver scans me over his shoulder a second longer than feels necessary. *Bare legs, middle of winter, that's not normal.*

I tug my skirt lower.

'Still staying at Mum and Dad's, then?' asks Nate.

'Until my place is ready—yeah.'

I look out of the window as the taxi pulls away, but I'm not really aware of the passing world or what I'm saying. My head is full of Lucas, of how he felt towards me, of what Nate did. And I don't want this conversation with my brother over the phone. I know I need to have it, but not now. I'm tired, and he's thousands of miles away getting a deal signed. It's not the right time.

'Don't do it, Eva'

'Do what?' I ask, even though I know.

'Go into business with him…bring him back into our lives.'

My anger erupts, spurred on by guilt at how we mistreated Lucas. The royal 'we'—the Beaumonts. And my brother is still sticking the knife in.

Remember, now isn't the time…

'*I'll* decide what's best for my product and for my business, Nate.'

'And what if he's doing this just to stir things? Have you thought about that?'

Christ, when haven't I? Isn't that why I'm terrified, in part…?

'He could screw you over just as easily as—'

'Nate.'

I hear his breath, heavy down the phone.

'Fine. But keep me posted, okay? And keep Dad in the loop? No nasty surprises.'

'No, no nasty surprises.'

Not like the one I just got, learning how you screwed Lucas over. Not that I was truly surprised.

'So, how is Hong Kong and the lovely Mrs Chan?'

He laughs down the phone at me and my body eases into the seat. 'Eva, I'm not kidding. The woman terrifies me…'

For the remainder of the cab journey he fills me in, and then quizzes me on what to buy Mum and Dad for

Christmas. The conversation turns easy, and it's the perfect distraction—until I let myself into the apartment, into the kitchen, and in my head I'm naked, with Lucas pressed into my back...

My body tightens on a shiver of heat, of longing, and I reach a hand to the cool surface of the worktop, dragging in a breath.

I'll never have enough of Lucas. He's the only man I've ever loved, the only man who's truly got under my skin. And now I've learned the truth. He's not the enemy my family painted him as for so long. *He's* the one who's been wronged.

Where does that leave us? Leave me?

Scared.

If I listen to my fear then I'll take his business off the table and run—because being around him and keeping my heart under wraps is impossible. And if I don't— if this love has chance to take hold again—what am I risking?

Everything.

There can be no future. Not with the past as it is.

But what if it could be changed? What if the air could be cleared? What if he could be welcomed back?

Was it even possible?

I feel a lightness creep its way in, see the future opening up with possibility...

There *has* to be a way. Mum and Dad are good people; they're controlling, overprotective, but *good* people. And Nate isn't himself—he hasn't been since the day he and Lucas went their separate ways. It has to be rooted in guilt, shame for what he's done, a desire to avoid Lucas and the memory of it all.

But surely if Lucas is willing to forgive, Nate can stop this whole *don't trust him* shit. He can take responsibility for what he's done and stop insisting that Lucas is on a revenge mission. Because I don't believe it. Not after all Lucas has said.

And he can't be lying. That photo isn't a lie. His desire for me can't be fake. So the rest has to be the truth too…

But what if it's not?

CHAPTER NINE

DESPITE TELLING LUCAS that our PAs would handle it, I'm still surprised when it comes to Friday and I've not heard from him.

I was so convinced he'd call. But then I didn't exactly leave him on fabulous terms. I gave him my warning that his deal was questionable and then ran off to deal with my family and the mess that is me, my feelings.

I've been trying to come to terms with both since— to come up with a plan, even.

It's less than three weeks to Christmas. Three weeks until the Beaumonts do what they do best and celebrate the season all cosied up at the family home. The family home Lucas was once a part of. And I want that again. More than anything.

I pull open my office door and Clare looks up with a smile.

'Do we have a new meeting scheduled with Waring Holdings yet?'

My cheeks flush a little and I damn my inability to stay cool.

If Clare notices, she's ever the professional and

doesn't comment on it. A few clicks of the mouse, a scan of the screen and then she's frowning.

'I don't see anything—should there be?'

'No… I mean, yes.'

She looks at me oddly and I shake off the madness. It's five p.m. on Friday. If his PA was going to get in touch she would have done so by now. Is he getting cold feet? Has talk of Nate given him cause to rethink?

Well, would you want to get back in bed with the Beaumonts after…?

Less of the bed, Eva.

'Eva?'

My eyes focus on Clare, my brain playing catch-up with what we were saying. 'Sorry, I expected his PA to get in touch to arrange one, but maybe he's expecting me to initiate it.'

It's possible. Unlikely, but possible.

She squints at me. 'Would you like me to do it?'

'Hmm…?'

Even Clare's professional mask is slipping now, at my dizzy behaviour.

'Would you like me to get in touch and arrange something?' she asks.

Would I?

My mobile starts to ring and I check my watch—*Dad.*

Great. No guessing what he wants to talk about.

I look back at Clare, but I'm not confused now. I'm fed up with being told what do, being controlled and manipulated into whatever action suits the Beaumonts.

This venture was meant to be my chance to break away and it still is.

'Yes, give Waring a call—see what you can work out.' I look back to my watch, still flashing at me. 'Sooner rather than later, Clare.'

'On it.'

'Thanks.' I turn back into my office and swing my door closed, bracing myself for Dad.

I take up my phone from the desk as the missed call alert appears and activate callback as I head towards the window and look out at the twinkling Christmas lights lifting the street below. They're beautiful, innocent, a real contrast to the chaos going on in my head.

The phone doesn't even complete a full ring in my ear.

'Evangeline.'

Now I'm five years old. The contrast between Lucas saying my name and my father is marked. 'Yes, Dad.'

'You've remembered who I am, then?'

My head nods of its own accord and a surprising smile lifts my lips. This is just how it is with my family—how it's always been—but I feel in control now, and it's different.

'I saw you a week ago, and it's not like we haven't spoken.'

'Yes, well… I just expected a call, you know… A status update on how things are…progressing…'

He sounds shifty. With good reason. 'You mean things in general or things with a certain someone?'

'Your brother called—he said you were seeing him.'

'In so much as it suits my business, yes.' Okay, so that's a lie. But it's not like I let Dad in on my sex life anyway.

'Evangeline, why would you *do* that? You know it's only going to cause ructions, and God knows what his true intentions are.'

'You sound like Nate.'

'You should listen to him—he knows better than most.'

'Really, Dad?' I can't stop the angry pitch of my voice. 'And how's that?'

'You *know* how.'

'Oh, that's right—Lucas did a runner when their company collapsed and now he's back to mess things up for me. Have I summed it up?'

My father is quiet on the other end of the phone and I see no need to rescue him. If he has a sound argument—the truth, even—I'll listen to it.

'Or shall we talk about how Nate did that dodgy deal all by himself?'

'You don't know what you're talking about—'

'Don't I?'

But I can hear the hesitation in his voice—can sense he's not as convinced as he's trying to make out.

'So Lucas *didn't* come to you after it all kicked off and tell you what Nate had done?'

'Yes, he did… But—'

'But you chose not to believe him. Lucas—a man who was always solid, trustworthy, dependable. Who doted on you as a father figure and balanced out Nate's crazy antics.'

'It's not that simple—'

'Isn't it? You said it yourself, Dad. They were yin and yang, Lucas kept Nate in check. And yet you were so quick to listen to your son, never mind that you destroyed Lucas.'

'I hardly think I destroyed him. He's hugely successful—a pillar of the business commun—'

'And what does that matter when he has no one to share that success with?'

My voice cracks and I purse my lips together, fighting back the well of emotion.

Dad is quiet. I want him to say he's sorry. I want him to tell Lucas he's sorry. But there's nothing.

'Speak to Nate,' I say, pushing him. 'Or I will. It's time he came clean.'

'It's in the past, Eva. Why do you want to go dragging it up now?'

'Because it affects the future—you know it does. And why should Lucas be tainted by it? We should *all* know the truth. Mum included.'

'But you know how your brother is… If we do this—'

'If we do this, *what*? He relapses?' I snap. 'Christ, Dad, he needs to take responsibility for it—he needs to grow up.'

'Maybe if Lucas hadn't abandoned the company—'

'*Don't*, Dad. You're still defending Nate over Lucas.'

'I just want you to be careful, honey. I don't want you hurt in some twisted attempt at revenge.'

My laugh is scathing. 'That's the *last* thing I need to worry about.'

'I'm not so sure…'

'I am,' I say, sounding more confident than I feel. 'This is *my* product, *my* company. I will make the best decision for both and see your investment paid back in full.'

'I don't care about getting the money back. All—'

'I *do*, Dad.' I want to be free. 'And I want you to speak to Nate.'

He's quiet again and I let the silence hang between us, pressing.

'Okay,' he says eventually. 'I'll try.'

'Don't just try—make him come clean. You're his father, for Christ's sake, he never should have lied to you in the first place.'

'No… I know.'

And there's something in the way he says 'I know'— *guilt*—that has me wanting more. I almost tell him that he should look at himself, too, to see why Nate was driven to do what he did, but I don't dare. I hope that in talking to each other it will come out anyway, and he'll shoulder his part in all of this.

It's a start, and it's as good a time as any to cut the call before he can backtrack. 'I have to go.'

'Evangeline, wait.'

'What is it?'

'Your brother gets back next week. We thought a family dinner would be nice.'

'Will you speak to Nate before that?' I ask, too eager to stop myself.

'Perhaps not before, but after—when the time is right.'

I want to ask exactly when he thinks that might be, but my dad is not a man to be pressed and I've already done plenty of that.

'When are you thinking of for dinner?'

'Friday—a kind of welcome home and pre-Christmas planning session. You know how your mother loves to plan for the festivities.'

I smile. It's instinctive. I love Christmas. I love my mother's obsession with it. And I love my family, no matter how they rile me. And now I have my father's assurance that he will talk to Nate I feel lighter, almost happy.

'Sure. I'll see you then.'

I hang up and head to the door just as someone raps on it. 'Yes?'

Clare walks in, eyes wide.

'What is it?' I ask.

'Erm…you're free this weekend, right?'

'Aside from some Christmas shopping I have planned, yes. Why?'

'Great, that's all I need to know.'

Lucas strides in as he speaks. *Lucas.*

'Thanks, Clare.'

He's dismissing my PA and I'm on another plane, I swear to God. My eyes rake over him, my brain disengaging over the mere sight of him. He's wearing a dark blue suit, his white shirt tie-free and distractingly open at the collar.

The door clicks shut. We're alone and there's so much I want to do with that—none of it conducive to work.

And didn't I just tell Dad I'm doing this for work? For work and to fix the past.

Liar.

'It's good to see you.'

He speaks again—not that he has much choice. I'm still struggling past the heart-shaped wedge in my throat.

'Evangeline?'

Better. So much better coming from him.

I smile and walk back to my desk, setting down my phone and leaning my hip against its edge as I look back to him. 'So, what's this talk of the weekend?'

I'm so damn curious my blood is pumping with it, excitement quick to follow.

'You questioned my ethics…'

My eyes narrow. 'Ethics?'

'You made some sweeping remark about crossing human rights lines.'

He's right. I did. But it was a fair—if unlikely—assumption based on the figures he presented.

'I have concerns, that's all.'

'And that's why I'm here.'

He clears his throat and shoves one hand into the pocket of his trousers, the other through his hair—*is he nervous?*

'I'm going to put your mind at rest.'

He's actually rather cute when he's nervous…

You're supposed to be talking work, Eva.

'How so?'

'My jet's on standby. I'm taking you to Singapore.'

Singapore? I straighten. *He can't be serious.*

'I can't just up and leave.'

'Seems you can.' He holds my eye, any trace of nervousness gone. 'You have no plans, you can shop in Singapore if need be and Clare has cleared your Monday too.'

'But—'

I break off. There's no reason for me to say no. In fact my body is screaming *yes*. With such force it's scaring me. I am so hooked on him, so keen...

Oh, yes, definitely scared. And excited. *Say yes.*

'Seems to me the best way to convince you of my upstanding ethics is to show you in practice—wouldn't you agree?'

'I...'

'And besides...it'll be fun.'

Fun. So much implied in that one word...

'Okay...' I say slowly, processing, considering...

'Great, the car's outside. We'll swing by your place en route to the airport.'

'Now?'

His grin is unhurried, and electrifying as fuck.

'Yes, now, Evangeline.'

I'm on my best behaviour. This is about convincing her to work with me.

But the way she keeps looking at me...the way her face lit up when she stepped onto the jet and asked if it was mine...

Impressing her is like a drug, I want to do it again and again and again. And, luckily for me, this trip is all about that.

The Beaumonts have money—serious money—but they don't have wealth like this.

'Can I get you something to drink, Mr Waring?'

I pull my attention from Eva, who's been exploring the cabin area since we hit cruising altitude, and look to Frederick, my on-call flight attendant. Ever efficient, polite and discreet.

'Please—champagne.'

Eva's eyes flick to me, widening.

'What?' I ask innocently.

'A bit extravagant, don't you think?'

We're on my private jet and champagne is what she deems 'extravagant'?

'No.'

Her smile is provocative as much as it is coy. 'Celebrating a bit early, aren't you?' she asks.

'No.'

She settles herself into a sofa, her hands reaching out to smooth along the upholstery—*yes, she's definitely impressed.*

'This has nothing to do with work and everything to do with a drink worthy of the company.'

She laughs and it ripples through me, heat tightening me up like a coiled spring. 'Some water, too, please, Frederick.'

'Of course, sir.'

He disappears, and Eva watches him go before looking back to me, her brow wrinkling. She's serious and happy all at once—speculative, if I had to put a word on it. But she's not wary...not like she was before.

'Are you hungry?' I ask.

It's almost nine in the evening and I know she's not eaten. We've been together since we left her office. And I've loved every second.

Something's changed since that night at my apartment—whether it's what I told her, or something else, she's different. She seems relaxed—*hell, I'm relaxed*. It's rubbing off on me, blurring the boundaries of this trip. Personal or business...?

Something flares inside. Something akin to hope.

'Ravenous,' she says.

My breath catches. *Jesus.*

It's an honest answer, perfectly platonic, but to my hyped-up body she might as well have begged me to screw her with that very sweet word. Frederick present or not.

And, speak of the devil, he appears, champagne in hand.

'Miss Beaumont.'

He offers her a glass and she takes it with a smile.

'Thank you.'

Frederick beams back at her. Frederick my professional and extremely impassive flight attendant. Yet another person who breaks character for her and they've barely shared two words.

I can't blame him either. Eva has this look in her eyes when she's relaxed that seems to encompass the world.

They're so bright, so caring, so captivating. And I'm hooked on them as I take my own glass.

'What has Andreges prepared for dinner?'

I barely hear as Frederick runs through the menu. I'm watching as Eva's lips part with growing surprise and, if the colour in her cheeks is any indication, with pleasure too.

'Wow,' she says when he finishes, 'that sounds fabulous.'

'I trust it's acceptable?'

Frederick is asking me, of course, but I'm still looking at her.

'Is it?' I ask.

Her smile fills the cabin, contagious as it sweeps us both. 'Acceptable? It sounds delicious!'

'Wonderful.'

Frederick clasps his hands together, still beaming. This is the most animated I've ever seen him.

'I will bring it through shortly.'

He glides away and silence descends. Her eyes are off me as she frowns into her champagne, and her switch from exuberant enjoyment to quiet introspection is so rapid I struggle to keep up.

Despite the cushioned leather I'm suddenly uncomfortable, and I shift in my seat, running a finger through my open collar. I can take a guess at what she's thinking about, but I don't want to go back to that. We've done the past. Now I want to look to the future.

'I spoke to my father,' she says, before I can think of a conversation-starter to stop her.

I drink my champagne but barely feel its chilling progression down my throat or even taste it. The Beaumonts make me numb. It's a defence mechanism—effective with all bar her. But I've come to accept that. I don't want to be numb with her. I like how alive she makes me feel.

'And...?'

'I told him he needs to get the truth out of Nate and acknowledge they did wrong by you.'

She sits straighter and brushes her free-flowing hair over one shoulder, all calm and controlled and breathtaking with it.

'I also told him to back off as far as my business goes. This is my decision—they have no say in it.'

I don't react, keeping my face deadpan even though inside my pride in her swells. The Evangeline of our youth would never have stood up to them.

'You said it just like that?' My lip quirks as I imagine it.

'Pretty much,' she says, and the glint in her eye hits me with the blue of her sweater. I love her in blue. Hell, I love her in every colour.

I realise she's staring at me, waiting for a response, and I ask carefully, 'How did they take it?'

She drinks her champagne and shrugs. 'Dad's still coming to terms with Nate's lies—he needs to hear it from him.'

I nod. 'And our potential working relationship?'

She doesn't look away. 'I think they're both of the opinion that you've got some devious plan to screw me over,' she says. She narrows her sights on me and leans forward slowly, provocatively, 'So, Mr Waring, *do* you have some wicked plan to take revenge?'

I have a thousand wicked wants in that second, with her lips slick with champagne and pouting at me. But I sense that, for all she jokes, this is important. I can't deny that I've thought about it, that there would be something just in that kind of revenge, my anger towards Nate bringing out the worst in me. But it's not what drove me to her.

'I'm a busy man, Eva. I don't have time to exact some ill-considered revenge.'

She cocks her head to one side, her teeth scraping over her lip as she quietly considers my words. 'Which brings me to my other question: Why come to me at all?'

I go to answer, but she continues.

'I know you want my product, that you want to join forces with me, and that's all perfectly acceptable. But *you*—why are you doing all the leg work? You must have a multitude of very capable employees to entrust with the task of gaining my business, of coming to the party, attending meetings, even taking me on this tour... But it's all you.'

'Why shouldn't I? The potential is huge, the competition for the work fierce. I wanted you to know I'm serious.'

'Wanted *me* to know, or my family?'

She leans back in her seat, crossing her legs over one another, and even though she's now wearing jeans, following a quick change at her home, the skinny fit of the fabric is doing nothing to help ease the appeal of those long, lithe legs I've traced with my mouth, my fingers...

'Why does it matter?'

I don't know why I ask it. A delaying tactic, I suppose. Because, as I've come to realise, there is one reason above all others that I came, and I'm not sure she's ready to hear it yet.

'You *know* it matters.'

'I didn't think it fair to send in one of my people when I wasn't sure how well my company would be received.'

She raises an eyebrow at me. Amused. 'And you thought your own physical presence would be preferable?'

I laugh. 'I wouldn't go that far.'

'No?' She toys with the stem of her glass, her eyes following the rotation of it in her fingers.

'I figured that if there was a personal block to our companies working together it was best I confronted it head-on and in person. I didn't expect...'

I trail off and her eyes lift to me.

'Expect what?' she asks.

'This.'

I'm not going to lie to her. I'm done with secrets, cover-ups.

'Ten years...' She smiles softly. 'Who would think something could flare up again so readily?'

I wonder if she means it. Is she genuinely surprised at this force determined to pull us together? Whatever the case, my body is already gearing up to pursue the suggestion in her gaze, regardless of my good intentions when we boarded.

'Indeed.'

My agreement is tight, loaded, and the silence that ensues is heavy.

She looks to the door through which Frederick disappeared. 'When do you think the food will arrive?'

I follow her line of sight, my body rigid as I read her intent. 'Soon.'

'Shame…'

I smile as I try to set my body to chill. 'I thought you were hungry.'

'Absolutely famished.'

'*Evangeline…*'

It's a warning. To her. To me.

'I'm guessing you're already a member,' she says, looking at me from under her lashes.

'A member?'

My heart is thrumming in my ears now, the warmth coiling through my body reaching breaking point. She takes a long, slow sip of the straw-gold liquid, her throat moving hypnotically, her little appreciative hum teasing me.

'Come on, Lucas, you're not *that* innocent.'

I swallow, hard. Of course I know to what she's referring. And there's a bed next door…ready to be used. But I don't want this to be about sex. Me and her. I want it to be about business. About convincing her I'm the right company for her. Not cloud it with this.

But then, after the way we parted, this is the last thing I expected to be heading off.

'Tell me…is it as amazing as they say at high altitude?'

She's still sitting out of reaching distance, but I feel her words like a caress over my cock, and a stream of erotic scenarios streak through my mind.

'They say it's to do with the dip in atmospheric pressure…' she practically purrs. 'The reduction in oxygen levels messing with your brain, making you feel more stimulated, intensifying the pleasure…'

She curves a hand over her upper thigh and I fight the urge to move, to cover her hand with my own.

'I wouldn't actually know.'

'With your reputation, you expect me to believe that?'

I laugh, projecting mock-offence. 'Why is it so hard to believe?'

'Come on, Lucas, you *own* this jet—don't tell me you haven't brought a date on it?'

'No, I haven't.'

I date women, sure. And I have connections around the globe. But they're connections, not relationships. They serve a purpose when I need it. The jet is simply my transport for work—it's not a social vehicle.

Not that I really *do* social.

'Give over. Once a player, always a player,' she murmurs into her drink.

I sense she's teasing me, but I don't like it.

Let it go.

I can't. It's the same reason I couldn't let her remark about human rights slide. I want her to see the good in me. And if not the good, then at least the truth.

'Is that how you see me?'

She lowers her glass to the side table and her eyes soften. 'Sorry. I didn't mean to insult you. It's just… you know. *All* those girls when we were younger…you and Nate were horrendous.'

She's not wrong. I remember it well. But I also remember the reason, and I want to tell her. But it will open me up, expose me.

My neck prickles. I'm not used to talking so much. Even though I want to tell her, there's a part of me that fears the power it will hand her.

And isn't that as bad as confessing the real reason I came to her personally instead of sending an employee?

But is it so bad if it's the truth?

'Look, it's okay, Lucas. You're not the only one playing the field.' Her cheeks colour and she waves a carefree hand. 'And, hey, you're a desirable bachelor. I'm not judging you. I'm just…you know…saying that if you had…'

She's babbling and flustered and I fucking love her for it.

I stop thinking. I sweep across the cabin and pull her with me onto the sofa, crushing her mouth with my own, swallowing her startled moan.

She moulds to me instantly, her kiss just as fierce, as hungry.

God, this feels right. Being here like this with her.

Totally wrapped in one another. I try to tell her, I need to tell her, and then I hear movement—

A trolley. Frederick. Christ.

I pull away from her and give her an apologetic smile. 'Time to satisfy that hunger of yours.'

She blinks at me, dazed. All hot and bothered and embarrassed at once, And then she turns to Frederick and musters a sheepish grin.

To his credit, he barely bats an eyelid. 'Dinner is served.'

He lays it out on the dining table before us. The smell wafts over to me, mixed in with the lingering scent of her still tingling my senses.

'Thank you,' I say, and he dips his head before turning and leaving once more.

I move to the table, retrieving our drinks as I do so, and wait for her to sit before I follow suit, placing her drink before her.

She raises it to her lips, her eyes locking with mine. I do the same. And this time I taste it. I feel the fine stream of bubbles dance over my tongue, taste the caramel, the hint of lemon...

It's exquisite.

As is she.

The perfect match, just as I told her.

And she deserves the truth. I need her to know.

'All those girls you saw me with...'

She takes up her cutlery and shakes her head softly. 'Don't worry about—'

'It was because of you.'

Her fingers still, her eyes return to mine. 'Me?'

Her frown is delectable. I want to lean over, kiss it away, trail kisses right down to her open lips.

'Yes, you.' I reach out, brushing my thumb across her cheek as I lose myself in her eyes.

'I was trying to prove to myself that I could look past you.'

'Past…me?'

'You were off-limits. I had to go elsewhere.'

It's so simple, so honest, but she doesn't seem to accept what I'm saying.

'It was a foolish notion,' I add.

She licks her lips and her cheeks heat beneath my palm. 'How so?'

'Because there's only one you.'

There—I've said it. It's out there.

Her lashes flicker, her eyes water. *Jesus, she's going to cry.*

'I…I don't know what to say.'

'Nothing. You need to eat. And then you need to sleep.'

She's staring at me as if I'll give her more, but I'm done with opening up. My body is tight with it.

Fear. That's what it is. Fear of where it puts us now. Because the one thing I'm sure of is that I love her. Still love her. And she loves her family. Her family who hate me.

I watch as she cuts up her food, but I sense that her mind is racing with what I've told her. Hell, mine is. What did I hope to gain? A sweeping confession of something similar from herself? And even if she had, then what?

The problem is I'm selfish. I have no one else. I only have to look out for me.

Which means I should be going after not just her business but her heart too, and saying to hell with the Beaumonts.

I should make her choose. Them or me.

I should.

But I can't.

She forks the food and places it in her mouth. Her shoulders relax, her lashes lower and then she smiles, pleasure ringing through her and pulling me in.

Screw the Beaumonts—make her choose.

CHAPTER TEN

DINNER IS INCREDIBLE. Fine dining at its best, all at forty-odd thousand feet in the air. It's almost too good to believe, but my taste buds are still zinging over the lemon tart I ate for dessert and I'm still crushing over the jet itself.

It's real.

I blame it on the designer in me. I've only seen a glimpse of the galley kitchen beyond the door behind me—all black and glossy, with crystalware on display in a high cabinet and accented lighting that you'd expect in a slick city apartment.

The cabin we're in features a plush sofa, seats that swivel and recline, a high-tech TV and sound system, and the dining table at which we sit is laid out like a high-end restaurant. All in colours designed to soothe and relax.

And I am *so* relaxed.

The flight is smooth; only the gentle hum of the engine, the dry air and the strange headiness that comes with flying remind me that we are truly on a plane.

This kind of luxury is beyond belief. I knew people

did this sort of thing—of course I did. I just never expected to be one of them.

And it truly does beg the question... *What would it be like?*

I look at him sitting across from me. He's checking his phone, his face serious and so goddamn sexy. It should be a crime to be this attractive, this distracting.

And the way he watched me through dinner... My body warms at the memory. He wants me as much as I want him. I know it. And who *wouldn't* want to experience an orgasm at altitude just to know if it's truly that good?

And just maybe the fizz is going to your head quicker than normal and your inhibitions have gone the way of your brain. Hmm...entirely possible... But do I care?

His eyes lift to mine and my breath catches, my pulse making a little trip of its own. *No.*

'All okay?' I say, amazed that I sound relatively normal.

'Yes.'

'Care to share?' I ask.

What the actual fuck?

His brow cocks and I want to slap myself. As if I have *any* right to know what he's up to on his phone. But it was supposed to be a flirtatious prompt—like *Hey, I'm interested.*

Oh, God.

The fizz and altitude have definitely gone to my head.

'Just catching up on messages and firing one off to the team in Singapore to confirm our arrival.'

I nod and automatically lift my wine glass. I do a mental recap: three glasses of champagne and a bit of red—*no more for you*—and put it down again.

'Isn't it early there?' I check my watch. It's half-ten at night, UK time. 'What is it? Eight hours ahead?'

'Yes.'

'So that makes it six-thirty…?'

My voice trails away. That look is back in his eye—that look that has salacious heat swirling in me so readily that I forget what point I'm even getting to.

'You should get some sleep.'

'Sleep?' Sleep is not what I'm thinking of. Far from it.

'Yes—you know…that thing babies hate, teens crave and us adults scarcely get enough of.'

I give a laugh, but it's tight with need. I know it is, and he does too, judging from the way his eyes drop to my mouth.

'Why break form, then? Sleep can come later…' I say.

The lights have been dimmed, the plates cleared away. Frederick is gone—dismissed until his next summons, I assume—and I'm curious to see what other thrills this plane has to offer.

I stand and step around the table. 'Tell me, Lucas, where do you sleep?' I walk around the cabin, my fingers brushing over the back of a chair. 'Here?'

To be fair it looks as comfy as any hotel bed, but he shakes his head, his jaw tense. It's as if he's fighting his instincts and I wonder why…

I look to the back of the cabin, to the closed door, and I know the answer before I ask. 'What about through there?'

I walk towards it and look at him over my shoulder. He's still seated, rooted, but his eyes follow me.

'May I?' I say, my fingers over the handle.

I move before he answers, sliding it open, and I can't stop the gasp that parts my lips. I shouldn't be surprised—not having already enjoyed the living space, glimpsed the kitchen. But I am.

It's incredible: sexy, dark, alluring. Much like its owner.

I sense him move and suddenly he's behind me.

'That bed just calls to me...' I murmur, taking in the mink throw, the cloud-like pillows and inviting duvet.

He laughs softly. 'Good, because you're sleeping there.'

I turn to him, my palm lifting to his chest, feeding off his warmth. I can't meet his eyes, though. I feel suddenly unsure, nervous of his answer despite all he's said. 'You've really never brought anyone else here?'

'No.'

'So I'm the first?'

'Yes.'

My tongue sweeps over my bottom lip and I feel his chest tighten beneath my palm, his breath brushing over my forehead.

'What are you thinking about?' I ask.

'I'm thinking you should get into bed,' he says, backing away a little. 'I'll sleep out here. We've a busy weekend planned, and this is all about our two companies working together. I want to keep us focused on that.'

I smile. My eyes are still lowered. He's trying to do what's right. Trying to maintain some form of professionalism and I love him for it. But I love the sexual undercurrent even more—the tightness in every word he speaks, the tension thrumming off his body.

'Is that why you kissed me earlier? To keep me focused on work?'

He clears his throat. 'I shouldn't have.'

I look up. 'Oh, yes, you should.'

I lift myself on tiptoes, my lashes closing, and he moves swiftly, his hands reaching out to grip my arms. 'Come on, Eva—bed.'

My eyes flick to his. 'You're coming with me.'

'No, this is *your* bed for tonight.'

I pout. Actually pout. Like some naughty child. He can't be serious. He's given me signs all evening that this is heading somewhere, that this isn't just about work.

And now he steps back out of the room while my cheeks burn.

'There's a bathroom through there—help yourself to anything you need, Frederick has already brought your suitcase in.'

'Lucas?'

I don't want to sound affronted. But I am.

Or am I tipsy? Is that what this is? Some drunken plea and he's saving me from myself?

My cheeks flame deeper and his smile is small, warm. 'Sweet dreams, Evangeline.'

He slides the door closed, leaving me alone, and I have to stop myself from striding after him and demanding he *do* something. Anything to see off this need he's evoked.

It's his fault.

Entirely his fault.

So why am I still loving his decency?

I flop onto the bed and am instantly cocooned in softness. The kind that makes every muscle in your body go weak, your brain quiet. *Bliss.*

He can have his way for now—his bed is an inviting compromise—but there are hours ahead. Many hours in which he can change his mind...

All he needs is the right kind of nudge.

I smile as I strip down to my underwear and climb beneath the quilt. I'll just give him a few hours of thinking he's won first...

I flick my phone over, face down on the table, and lean back into my seat.

Ignore it. Ignore him.

But Nate's text burns into me:

Leave her the fuck alone.

And she really thinks that talking to her family, her father talking to Nate, is going to fix this?

Like hell it is.

I grit my teeth and close my eyes, riding my shoulders into the soft upholstery, seeking comfort, seeking the blissful ignorance of sleep. But my conscience laughs at me. There's no way sleep will be forthcoming when I know she's lying in the room next to me. Wanting me.

I know she's pissed off with me. My rejection has goaded her. And I can't blame her—not when it comes so soon off the back of that kiss, when all my good intentions disintegrated, incinerated in the heat of a need that won't shift.

I'm torn between doing what I want and encouraging her down a path that she might regret.

If I'd told her one of my messages was from Nate—the first message I've received from him since I changed my number all those years ago—would she still have tried to jump me?

It's a question I can't stop tossing around—have been for the last two hours, since closing the door on her.

I swing from wanting to send an equally angry retort to her brother and then taking what's on offer in my bed, to protecting her from herself…from me. I'm not blind to the anger that still bubbles beneath the surface. The resentment. It fizzes in my blood at every mention of her family. But my need for her, my love, swamps it.

Or maybe it feeds it?

Maybe there is an unconscious need to have what I shouldn't—to have what pisses them off the most.

I force my hands to relax and shimmy my shoulders further back—*sleep, just sleep.*

Logic tells me to get the deal signed, get her in my life and *then* go after more. Not to jeopardise the business by encouraging a relationship I'm not sure she can accept. Not when her family are so against it.

But the alternative—the platonic route—is impossible. No matter how short-term. I need her as much as I need my next breath.

And then I hear it: the soft glide of the door.

My fingers twitch; my chest tingles.

'Lucas?'

Her voice is soft, whisper-like. Has she just woken up?

I try to appear asleep. I can't begin to imagine how she looks right now, dishevelled by sleep. Or, if she hasn't slept, from tossing and turning. Either way my body heats at the very idea.

'Are you awake?'

Her feet pad towards me and I try to even out my breath, relax. The room goes quiet and I know without looking that she's studying me.

One breath in. One breath out. In—

Her fingers brush gently over my forehead, taking back my fringe, and then her lips are there, soft, caressing.

'Lucas…'

Oh, God.

Her fingers slide down over my front and I realise how stupid playing asleep is. Awake, I can stop her. Awake, I can stop the progress of her fingers…

'Lucas, I know you're awake.'

My lips curve in a lazy smile. 'Not one to be easily fooled, are you?'

'No.'

'What gave me away?'

I open my eyes to meet hers. She's so close I can inhale her scent, feel the warmth of her body, and that's when I realise she's naked, with the low light of the cabin hinting at every glorious curve. *Fuck.*

'This.' She rakes a nail over my hardness, and my eyes and body feast on the simple stroke.

Sure enough, even in this light there is no denying how awake I am—awake and very much under her spell.

'You're supposed to be asleep—'

She grips me, and my words become a groan as I shift within her grasp.

'*Eva.*'

'The way I see it…' She runs her hand over me, and heat rushes to greet her touch. 'It will be near enough evening when we get to the hotel. There'll be time for sleep then.'

There is no hotel, but I'm damned if I can correct her. I'm trying to focus through a heavy haze of lust. Trying to hang on to what's right.

My fingers bite into the upholstery of my seat and my thighs tremble as I press into it, away from her, but she has me. I should extract her hands, make her move away, but I can't even do that.

'You don't like being told what to do?'

She shakes her head, and her teasing lips curve into a smile as she lowers her head to my ear. 'Especially when I want something as much as I want you.'

She trails her hot mouth across my jaw as she hooks her leg over me, spreading her heat over my erection.

'And I can feel you want me too.'

She rides against me and I'm back in that kitchen, with my cock getting the better of me.

Now I can move. I grip her hips, steadying her, halting her.

She pouts down at me. 'Don't be a spoilsport.'

Christ, if only...

I force an arrogant smile. 'You wouldn't want Frederick to hear, would you?'

Her eyes flick briefly in the direction of the kitchen. 'Worried I'm going to make a noise?' she asks.

She tries to move in my grasp and my hold tightens. She's a minx. An electrifying, dizzying minx. And suddenly I have the desire to do something extreme. Something that will stick the finger up at Nate. Something that will put me firmly in control and to hell with my good intentions.

'Come.' I lift her away from me and take hold of her wrist, striding to the bedroom before the lustful haze can lift and common sense can prevail. We make it to the bedroom. 'On the bed.'

She bites into her lip and lowers herself down onto it, every bend of her body, each slip of her hands over the duvet intentionally seductive.

'I like you like this,' she purrs.

Holy fuck.

I pull my gaze away, stripping off my clothes as she watches me. Not until I'm naked and have the cupboard that contains what I need open do I turn to her, the scarlet strip of silk in hand. A tie. One of my finest.

She looks from it to me, her brows raising. 'And what do you intend to do with *that*?'

She's provoking me and my cock fucking loves it. *Too much.*

I turn back and take out another tie. I need the second one to keep her under control—to keep *myself* under control. She's too efficient at tipping me over. Her hands, her body, her mouth—all dangerous.

I stalk towards her and she glides back on the bedcovers, her eyes pulling me in, her lips parted, anticipation in her breath.

'Have you ever been gagged?'

Her eyes flare as she shakes her head.

'Another first, then.'

'Yes.'

She leans up towards me, offering herself, accepting, and heat sears my gut. So much for keeping it under control.

I wrap the tie around her mouth, my eyes on hers as I gently tighten it. Her trust, her desire, her... *Her what? Love?* Hell, it looks like love. It looks like how I feel.

A very different heat swells, close to my heart, and with it comes that same edge—*fear*.

I can't deal with that right now.

I tug the strip of cloth tight, the sound of silk on silk a sharp whisper before softening as I tie it into a bow and lean back to take her in.

Her eyes are wider and her nose flares as she

breathes. Her cheeks flush pink and her lips form an erotic O as she tests the binding with her teeth.

'Okay?' I ask, even though I can see her answer. Her eyes blaze, her nipples are tight, her breasts flush the colour of her cheeks and I know if I dipped my fingers between her legs I'd feel it too.

She nods, a small sound quivering in her throat.

'Good. Hands?' My voice is tight with the command and dutifully she straightens up to offer them out.

I wrap the silk over her wrists, tying them together. She watches every move I make, her breath rasping over the gag, goosebumps prickling over her skin. She is so fucking sexy I'm starting to worry that just the sight of her is going to tip me over.

'Lie back.'

I help her down and raise her hands over her head, the tip of my erection nudging at her stomach as I move over her. She purposely arches into me, caressing me further. *Jesus.*

I fasten the tie-ends to the bar that decorates the bookshelf above the headboard and then back away to kneel over her, drinking in her naked beauty, willing her to be powerless and all mine.

She wriggles and whimpers, begging me for something, and I smile as she opens her legs to encase me, to draw me in. She's so wet… Her need glistens in the low light and I take pity. Just a little.

I reach forward and run my thumb up her slickened seam.

She cries into the tie, working her body against my

touch, and heat assaults my cock, pre-cum beading at its tip. It's goddamn erotic, having her like this, at my mercy, and I want to draw it out.

I climb off the bed and she moans after me, eyes pleading.

I take a fresh glass from the nightstand and head to the kitchen. Opening the freezer, I fill the glass with ice then return to her, my eyes lazy as they trail over her flushed skin.

She writhes towards me, her body outstretched, her whimpers begging, and then she spies the glass and stills, her eyes widening.

I lower myself to the bed, glass in hand, and she watches as I scoop out one ice cube and pop it into my mouth, rolling it around my tongue. She crosses her legs, her thighs clamped together, and I know she's feeding *that* ache. The same one that's throbbing through me for release as I move on all fours above her.

I drop my head to her neck slowly, teasingly, and I work my icy tongue over her skin, both cube and flesh caressing. Her breath hisses around the gag, her moans teasingly trapped.

I trail around to her front, to the hollow of her throat, where I dip and release the cube. It melts over her skin, where her pulse is beating a crazy tempo.

I take up another cube, running it down her front and beneath one breast. Her breath hitches and her body arches, her every reaction feeding my own. I work it in circles, getting steadily closer to where her nipple tightens.

I lock onto her eyes as I trace around the rose-pink bud. She shudders with a moan, turning her head into the pillow. I move to her other breast, teasing her with the ice, and then my lips drop to the well-worked nipple, my warm mouth a heated contrast.

Her body becomes tense, her legs wrap tightly over each another.

I know she's close, but not yet...

I rise up onto my knees and trail a fresh cube down her front, letting it rest in her belly button, where the ice water pools as she wriggles. Her eyes are glazed with lust, heavy and captivating, as she watches me part her legs.

I kneel between them, taking hold of the cube, and trace soft, light circles from her navel to the strip of hair. She is rigid now—ready, waiting—and as I tease her apart with the frozen edge she cries in her throat, her head thrown back.

I stroke the cube over her so lightly my touch is hardly there, but it's enough. I can see it in her heightened colour, in the way her breath is ragged over the silk.

I circle her clit, gently caressing, watching her writhe for more. Her fingers claw in their binding, and her muscles are tight. I know that with one suck of my mouth she'll be gone.

She lifts her head and looks to me, desperate, the crazy undulation of her hips begging. I toss the ice and grab her legs, lifting her to my mouth. I'm not soft, gentle, delicate. I'm rough, desperate, eager.

I claim her as my heart wants to. I drink from her. I dip inside her warm haven and then retreat, grazing her with the flat of my tongue as I slide all the way up.

The moment I strike her clit, her body spasms out of control. She's coming, her screams muffled and carnal and snapping my restraint. I flip her over, twisting her binding with the move, and lift her hips to meet me as I thrust, burying myself deep.

Her tight, wet heat closes around me—so mind-obliterating, so new. She pushes back on her knees, her wrists pulling at the silk tie, demanding more.

But then I still as the unfamiliar sensation strikes a second's clarity—*condom*.

'Shit.'

I grip her hips to stop her—to stop me.

She throws me a look over her shoulder, her pleading whimper threatening my resolve.

'Protection,' I grind out.

She shakes her head, rocking her body in my hold, clamping her pussy around me. She's telling me no. And, hell, I know I shouldn't—but, Christ, I know I'm safe, and I trust her.

And, oh, my God, she's pumping me. Back and forward again, her gorgeous body riding me, milking me. Heat rips through my thighs, my gut, my cock, and I'm thrusting hard and fast. There's nothing delicate about it. I'm fucking her. My hands bite into her skin, her moans are wild, and I want more from her, louder...

My thighs slap against hers. I take hold of her arse and grip it tight. I rub at the plump flesh and test the surface with the flat of my palm. She looks at me, daring me to do it, her eyes glinting, and I spank her, the slap mixing with the heady sound of her cry.

I do it again. My blood pulsing with the crazed heat of it. Of letting go. No control. No nothing. Just me and her.

I feel like I'm punishing her. Some crazy kind of punishment for the sins of her family. But I can't help it. And she's taking it all, giving as good as she gets. It's messed up, but I can't stop.

And then I'm coming, pleasure streaking though my limbs, frenzied and out of control, and she's there with me, her body spasming around me. My cry is so loud the whole jet will hear, but in that second I can't care.

I only care for her. And it feels right. *So* right.

Fuck Nate. Screw the Beaumonts. She's mine and I'm keeping her.

CHAPTER ELEVEN

I THOUGHT THE plane was impressive. I truly did. But now I'm standing in the penthouse of a skyscraper—our home for the next two nights—and I'm starting to forget what reality looks like.

I have a suspicion that Lucas owns this place. The private elevator to which he has access, the respectful greeting of the staff, the similar decor to that in his London apartment... There's just something about it that's all him.

And now I have it to myself. He's gone out on some work errand, leaving me with strict instructions to call Room Service for food and get some sleep.

But, seriously, how do you sleep when you're surrounded by this?

I twirl on the spot, my eyes tracing a spiral staircase that looks as if it's been carved out of a solid marble block, the mezzanine gallery that leads off to the bedrooms, and the outside area that I've only just glimpsed. I know there's a pool out there, just waiting to be used.

My stomach growls, reminding me of his orders.

But Room Service? Really? When Singapore by twilight awaits? No way.

As Lucas is already learning, I might have followed instruction well as a child, even as a teen, but no more.

I also have this bubble of nervous energy inside me, and being surrounded by something that is so entirely *him* is too distracting.

I rub my wrists. The flesh still tingles where he tied me, and the bubble balloons. Nervous energy. *Need*, more like. Need and so much more...

Time to go out.

I lift my clutch from a sofa that could seat at least ten and head out to the lift area, where I stop in my tracks. There's a glass wall alongside the elevator that I didn't see before. I was too wrapped up in Lucas and in following him inside. Now my jaw drops as I take in the sight beyond the glass. A bright red Ferrari and a vibrant blue Porsche stare back at me. I can't even hazard a guess at how high this rooftop penthouse sits, but surely too high for this, an *en suite* garage.

And the cars... I *love* cars. I have a Porsche too— it's my one real indulgence. But it's clear to see, even from this distance, that his is custom-made everything. Unique to him.

Unique *as* him.

I roll my eyes at my heart, which is getting so carried away, and continue to the lift, using a touchscreen to beckon it. Of course it opens immediately, as if it anticipated my request.

I scan my clothing in the lift mirror: skinny pants and a deep blue silk cami. It'll do. And I step in.

It takes me a few tries to navigate the touchscreen inside, and it occurs to me that I don't have a clue how to get back in. There will be some code—some pass that I need. But I tell myself it's fine, I'll speak to the lovely staff we saw on the way in. Nothing is insurmountable.

It's exactly what I'm planning on doing when the doors open and I step out into the vast lobby. Instead I'm frozen, my feet stuck to the glossy white floor.

The thing about Lucas is that he stands out. Even more so in Singapore. And there he is, in the middle of the bustling lobby, with a lady. A tall, statuesque Asian woman who is all poise and elegance, exotic and captivating.

My teeth grit and my heart clenches in my chest.

Business—*she's* business?

The past rips through me: Lucas the player, all those girls, the women since… *This woman.*

And he told me it was *me*! That *I* was the reason there'd been so many. And I believed him.

My body overheats. I'm not only hurt, and embarrassed over my foolishness, I'm *livid*.

He moves, and for the first time I see he has a red box under his arm. He hands it to her and she beams, leaning in to peck him on the cheek. I see the intimacy of the gesture, see her stroke the box affectionately, and I've had enough.

I stride forward. I don't know what I'm going to say but I'm not letting him think he can get away with this.

But you're not together. You're not in a relationship. This trip is about business for him. You're the one who turned it into more.

No, *he* turned it into more when he tied me to his bed, when he screwed me—

Oh, God, don't think about that now.

He cups her elbow and I see they're about to move off. I'm almost upon them and it's as if he senses my approach. His head turns and his eyes are on me. They narrow before they lift and he smiles. *Actually smiles.*

'Evangeline, you're supposed to be getting some rest.'

I pull myself up in front of him, hating how hot my cheeks feel and how the beautiful exotic creature with him balances *his* beauty so spectacularly. Even now, as she studies me with open curiosity, I acknowledge that she is perfect for him.

'I wanted to go out to eat,' I say. I turn to her, holding out a hand. 'Hi. I'm Evangeline Beaumont.'

'I know exactly who you are.'

Even her voice is exotic, captivating. She smiles at me, her eyes alive with appreciation, and I feel my heart stutter, confusion hot on its tail. She takes my hand and shakes it softly, her delicate perfume wafting up to me, and suddenly I feel dizzy.

'I have been so eager to meet you.'

'You have?' I retract my hand, my frown impossible to prevent.

'Yes, of course—to work with you would be such a pleasure.'

'Go easy, Maylene, she hasn't agreed yet.'

My eyes dart between them both, my brain too slow to play catch-up.

'Sorry...' Lucas says, gesturing between the goddess and I. 'Eva, this is Maylene—she heads up operations for me out here. And, as Maylene says, she knows exactly who you are.'

He smiles at me, so proud, and I feel it all the way to my toes. As well as feeling the wash of shame at how quick I'd been to misjudge the situation.

His brows draw together and I know he's reading me. Reading my *faux pas*. I need to cover it. *Quick.*

'It's lovely to meet you,' I say. And now I need to leave, before I humiliate myself further.

My eyes drop to the box in her hands and up close I can spot the famous Fortnum & Mason label, see a glimpse of mince pies through the clear square on its top.

'Mince pies?' I'm so surprised it just comes out.

'Ah, yes,' she coos. 'You *can* get them here, but it's never the same. It's my naughty indulgence—we can't be good all the time, hey?'

She winks at me and my cheeks flare. My 'naughty indulgence' is currently looking at me as if I'm the most intriguing specimen he's ever seen.

'I'll let you get on.'

'No, wait.' She looks to Lucas. 'It seems a little unfair that we go and enjoy the best curry Singapore has to offer and leave Evangeline to do her own thing.'

'I don't want to bore her with work, and she's supposed to be resting,' says Lucas.

Maylene rolls her eyes at me. 'And who are you? Her mother?'

I laugh. I like her. 'I'm *so* glad you said that.'

Lucas looks to us both. 'If you're going to gang up on me, I'm not going anywhere.'

'I have a feeling we'd get along fine without you,' I tease him. 'And, as it happens, I *love* curry.'

We look at him pointedly and then it occurs to me that maybe he doesn't want to discuss work in front of an outsider.

I forget my teasing for a moment. 'Unless you need to talk in confidence?'

Maylene waits for Lucas to reply and he gives a shrug. 'I guess you're here to see how we operate, so it can't hurt for you to sit in.'

'Great!' we say in unison, and her friendliness and Lucas's easy inclusion of me buries the dregs of my embarrassment and we head out into the evening.

A car is waiting for us. Of course it is. Like everything with Lucas, it's slick and high-end.

And I am totally swept up in it. In him.

If I really concentrated I'd hear my phone vibrating, my watch attacking my wrist with an incoming call. I'd also hear my eighteen-year-old self trying to issue warning after warning.

Don't get in too deep. Not yet.

But I'm having too much fun.

The food was good. The company exceptional.

Maylene and Eva hit it off. It's no surprise. They're

both intelligent women with personalities to match. And, of course, when they're together they can unite and rib me better. *Better for them.*

It's late when we get back. As the lift doors open into my suite Eva's already sweeping forward, confident in the new space—not like when we first arrived and she followed in my shadow.

She turns to face me now, her smile wide, her eyes alive, and she waves a hand at the exposed garage that's lit with LED spots from the floor. It's flash, but I love it.

And I know she does too.

Eva has always loved her cars. One type in particular. And I know it's drawing her eye now...

'*That* is impressive.'

'Are we talking about the feat of engineering required to get them up here or the cars themselves?'

'Both.' She beams. 'How do you get in?'

A few taps to my phone and the glass door slides up. '*No way.*'

And here I go again. Impressing her. Getting high on it.

She glides forward, her touch delicate as she strokes the red bonnet of my Ferrari. Normally I'd cringe—and if she was any normal woman I would—but I know Eva and I know she loves this particular car. I knew it when I bought it, and think of her every time I get in it. Maybe I've always secretly dreamed of this moment.

'Trust you to own one.'

She looks at me over the hood and tests the door handle. It opens, and she gives a giddy squeal before she drops inside. I'm grinning like a fool as I watch her, but there's no stopping it.

She settles herself in, her hands flexing around the wheel, and I join her, climbing into the passenger seat.

'It's no ordinary Ferrari, is it?' she asks.

'Ordinary?' I raise my brow at her. 'No Ferrari can be classed as *ordinary*.'

'True—but come on, tell me. What have you changed?'

I laugh at her eagerness. I miss this. Having her to share everything with. Just like we used to. It's nice. Really nice. I sit back in the seat and give her the low-down, watching the way her hands caress the interior, feeling her excitement build my own.

'She's a beauty.'

'That she is,' I say, and I'm looking at her—all her— and she knows it.

She meets my eyes, her smile softening as she places the back of her hand over her mouth and stifles a yawn. I feel it too—jet lag creeping in.

'Come on. Let's get you to bed.'

'Us,' she says. 'Let's get *us* to bed.'

Us. I love how that sounds. My body warms over it as I climb out of the car and walk around to help her up. She takes my hand and folds into my side as we walk out of the garage. I set the glass sliding back into place and make for the staircase.

She pulls on my arm to stop me as she kicks off her shoes, and then we're moving again and I'm thinking about sleeping. Sleeping and logistics.

'I had the spare room made up for you.' It feels ridiculous even as I say it and her laugh confirms it.

'You *know* I'm not going to use it, don't you?'

My smile is easy. 'I didn't think so.'

'Sweet of you, though.'

She hangs off my arm and rubs her cheek against my shoulder, almost catlike and loaded with affection. My heart squeezes in my chest.

Where is this heading? Am I a fool?

We reach my bedroom and she pulls away from me, heading for the bed that takes centre stage. She starts to strip as she walks and my throat tightens. But it's not all lust. There's a sense of her belonging here, a sense of comfort. And the fact that she clearly feels it too isn't lost on me.

I follow suit, taking off my jacket and unbuttoning my shirt. I don't remember ever doing this. Bringing a woman home and just undressing as if it's a nightly thing. In fact, I can probably count the number of women I've had in here on one hand.

I sit on the edge of the bed, stripping off my shoes, my socks. I feel her weight as she slips onto the bed too, the quilt shifting as she lifts it and slides under. The warmth that's been setting up camp in my chest since I came back into her life swells inside me.

I stand to unbutton my trousers and strip both those and my underwear away in one swoop, tossing them to the side.

'Do you always sleep naked?' she murmurs, her words drawn out and low.

I look at her as she blinks at me, her eyes heavy. The quilt is pulled to her chin and a pillow cocoons her head. She looks comfortable and inviting all at once.

'Yes.'

I smile and climb in beside her, careful not to let the air-conditioned draught in too much. Immediately she scoots over, resting her head on my chest, and my smile grows as I wrap my arm around her and hold her there.

'Lucas…?'

'Hmm…?'

'Don't you get lonely?'

I flinch and mask it with a shrug; her simple question has cut deep. 'I'm too busy to get lonely.'

She shakes her head. 'I don't believe you.'

She sounds strange, remorseful, so different from how she's been up until now, and I find I'm struggling for words. Too busy fending off the truth.

'You don't really have anyone—thanks to my family.'

Oh, God. Too close.

My gut writhes as I squeeze her shoulder. I'm aiming to reassure, but I can't speak past the chill.

She presses a kiss to my chest and turns her head to rest her cheek over my pec.

'I'm so sorry,' she whispers, and I feel a damp trickle over my skin—she's *crying*.

'Evangeline…?'

Oh, God, don't cry, baby.

'I'm so sorry.' She shakes her head again, her breath rasping. 'You don't deserve it—you don't deserve how my family has treated you. You don't deserve any of it.'

I turn her onto her back and gaze down into her face. Her eyes are clamped shut, tears escaping to trail down her face.

I press a kiss to her brow. 'Evangeline, look at me.'

She doesn't.

I lightly kiss the bridge of her nose. 'Please?'

Her lashes flutter open.

'You have nothing to be sorry for.'

I seal my words with another kiss, ending any denial with the gentle pressure of my mouth. I only want to comfort her, to make her happy again, but as her body curves into mine her nakedness draws me in, and my body stirs, my heart warms.

'Make love to me,' she whispers against my lips, hooking her legs around my hips, opening herself to me.

Something inside me eases, like a balm being smoothed over old wounds. I trust her—heart, mind and soul.

Make love to me...

Always.

I press home and in one swift move she surrounds me. Comfort, love, light. Everything I could ever want, ever need, is here...right now.

And I won't let anyone take it away.

Not Nate. Not her father. No one.

CHAPTER TWELVE

I AM BLISSFULLY COSY. Wrapped in the most luxurious quilt, my limbs entwined as I cuddle it to me.

But I'm alone.

My senses come alert. I'm not worried, though. He's here somewhere. The heady scent of fresh coffee is in the air and I can hear movement somewhere in the distance.

I open my eyes, blinking against the sunrise that fills the room with a golden glow. It's breathtaking, lighting up the sea and the sky beyond the glass, and I'm basking in it. I roll over and stretch, loving how my body still tingles after everything we have shared since we left London.

I smile and a little kick of glee erupts inside me. This is too good to be true.

But it is true.

And once I get my family in line it could be perfect.

My eighteen-year-old self is becoming an increasingly distant memory, her warning just as weak.

I leap out of bed and the sound of water breaking reaches me—*the pool*. I imagine him almost naked, his muscles rippling as he moves through the water, and my body sighs over the image.

I dip to collect his shirt from the floor and slip it on, heading in his direction. My pulse is already dancing, but as I step outside it skitters with my intake of breath.

The pool is outstretched before me, filling half of the long roof terrace. Two draped cabanas, a string of sun-beds and many decorative plants flank it on one side; on the other is the view. And there he is, gliding through the water, his back to me. A strip of black fabric sits tight over his behind and the rest is bare for me to enjoy.

I'm quiet as I pad out. I don't want to disturb his front crawl, and his perfect form delivering stroke after stroke is mesmerising. But of course he's nearing the end. At any moment he will turn and see me.

I lower myself to the edge and sit down, my toes test-ing the water. It's warm and I sink my legs in, swirl-ing them around as he disappears under the water and executes a perfect turn. Like a professional. Of course, that's Lucas all over…perfecting everything.

His head breaks the water and he flicks his fringe over—and that's when his eyes light on me, his smile wide and squeezing my heart tight. He picks up pace and reaches me before I can finish a breath, flicking his hair again, his smile sending butterflies loose.

'Morning, sleepyhead.'

He presses his palms into the pool edge either side of me and lifts himself effortlessly to plant a kiss on my lips. Water drips from him onto the shirt, down its opening, over my thighs, my skin alive to every patter.

'Sleep well?'

He drops back and I lean over to stroke his jaw, his stubble teasing at my fingertips. 'Very…'

'Thought you might.'

His grin tells me he's reliving the night and my body heats.

'I could get used to seeing you in my clothing.'

His eyes trail hot and heavy down my body, exposed save for the single fastened button at my waist.

'What time do we need to leave?' I ask. I'm already thinking about delaying and joining him in the pool. The water looks so inviting, and as for its single occupant… *mmm…*

'After breakfast. The coffee should be ready.'

I stroke my feet up his sides and he rests his hands over my thighs, making no attempt to move.

'Are you wanting a swim?'

'I didn't bring my costume.'

His smile turns wicked. 'It would be a waste anyway.'

And then he's pulling me in, shirt and all, his lips gentle as they find mine, his fingers in my hair combing, caressing.

I sigh into his mouth. 'Your shirt will be ruined.'

'I'll buy another.'

His lips turn urgent as he pulls it apart, the button disappearing somewhere on the pool-bed, his hands rough on my body as he caresses every curve, my breasts, my nipples. He presses me back against the wall, his groan of need echoed in my own.

I slip my hand inside his shorts and he bucks into my fingers—obedient, eager. I pull him out and, weightless in the water, lift my legs around him, positioning him so he thrusts, hard, deep, my slickness making it so easy, so welcoming.

He leans back, his face taut with desire, and he cups my arse with one hand, his free hand coming to rest over my pelvis, his thumb dipping to caress my throbbing clit.

God, yes.

He's circling over me, moving in me, and I stretch my arms out over the poolside, holding myself steady for his every move. It's electrifying, with the warmth of the rising sun and the water lapping over my exposed breasts an added thrill, and I'm coming in seconds, wave after wave racking my body.

I cry out, his name bursting from me, loaded with everything I feel. *'Lucas...'*

Tears prick the backs of my eyes, happiness welling so fierce, and I hear him join me.

His *'Evangeline!'* tips the tears over and I reach out to hook my hands around his neck, pulling myself tight against him as he pulses within me.

I want to tell him I love him. I want to so much, but something stops me. The rejected eighteen-year-old girl still hanging on? Or the fear of going through the same all over again?

And then there's my family and the rift I've yet to fix. Their suspicion that his motives aren't as innocent as he's made out. But I can't believe that. I won't.

'I could get used to good mornings like this,' he murmurs against my hair, his fingers stroking my nape.

I nod. It's all I can manage.

'Ready for some breakfast now?'

I rub my face against his chest, hiding my tears before I look at him. I don't want him to question them.
Because I *am* happy. In that moment I really am.

I can deal with the rest later.

'Absolutely.'

Breakfast is perfect. A selection of pastries, fresh fruit,
juice and coffee. But it's the company that truly makes
it: *him*.

And as we tour his business that day he's in his element. Hell, so am I.

What he's achieved isn't to be sniffed at. It's incredible. He's maximising the skilled workforce Singapore
is renowned for, and not only that—he's keeping them.
His staff turnover is lower than any competitor, and
when I quiz him on his costs and how he manages it
he has an answer for it all.

His *is* the right company for me to go into business
with. He can give me everything I need to break out on
my own. I wouldn't be beholden to him *or* my family.
As far as business goes it would be all me. That part
has nothing to do with sex, or love. It's about doing the
right thing for the product, showing I can really *do* this.

We talk not only to his managers, but to his work-
ers too. They show me the clean, comfortable hous-
ing the company provides, and they tell me about the

subsidised bills and all the amenities, which include a park area for children, a sports centre, a nursery. They tell me how Waring Holdings puts other big corporations that function in the vicinity to shame, and how people come flocking to work here. They tell me how his company has effectively saved them—*saved* them.

It's crazy to believe it, but I've seen reports from other companies around the globe—the undercover news articles, the suicides. It's exactly what I was worried about when I flagged the human rights issues at him.

But now he's more than assured me of his ethics—he's made me fall in love with him all the more. He's not only given these people jobs, he's given them homes, good lives to live and enjoy. In return for their fantastically skilled work he's given them the respect of a fantastic working environment.

It's so perfect. So Lucas.

I think of his easy relationship with Maylene, of the mutual respect so evident between them, and the report he's given me on what his company can achieve. He's the right choice. I trust his company. I trust *him*.

By the time we arrive back at his home that night I am sold. And he knows it. I can see it in his grin as he pulls open the cupboard for wine glasses.

'Red? White? Or am I permitted champagne now?'

I shake my head with a laugh. 'I haven't agreed to anything.'

'Your face tells me all I need to know… Come on—admit it. You were impressed!'

My smile is fit to burst. 'Perhaps.'

'Champagne it is.' He takes out two glasses and hunts out a bottle. 'Let's take it to the roof—the view is amazing this time of night.'

The view is amazing right now...

He's so handsome in his charcoal-grey suit, with his white shirt now open at the collar, his tie undone. I could hook my fingers through the ends and pull him in...forget the champagne...

'Come on,' he says.

Spoilsport.

I let him lead the way up to the roof and then I get it. The view by night *is* spectacular and he wants me to see it—he's still trying to impress me.

He places the bottle and glasses on a low table beside one of the draped cabanas and strips off his jacket and tie, tossing them on the foot of the double bed beneath before sitting down at its edge.

'You going to stay there all night or are you going to join me?'

'In a bit...' I say it teasingly, but if I get on that bed there's no way I'm looking at the view.

Instead I walk around to the other side of the cabana and hook my arm around the pole at the end, my eyes on the glittering lights of Marina Bay, the Gardens and their futuristic bubbles. It really is a sight to behold.

And then music starts flooding the bay and lights dance.

'What is *that*?'

He gives me a grin as he lifts the bottle and starts to unwrap the foil. 'You'll see.'

I look back out to the bay and see laser strobes hit the sky, coming from the ship-like rooftop of the structure across the water. They dance with the music, and the spectacular pods of what I know to be a shopping plaza below light up in tune, bouncing off the water. It's incredible, and I'm so transfixed I don't realise he's moved until he's alongside me, holding out a glass.

I take it blindly, not wanting to miss a second. 'Thank you.'

'A free light show...' He bends to my ear as he says it and a heated shiver travels up my spine. 'What more can you possibly want?'

'Free?' I laugh softly. 'You really are spoiling me.'

His return laugh is husky, low, and I bite into my lip.

'There'll be another one later,' he says. 'They're on every night. The tourists go crazy for it. I've had a place here for a year and I still try to catch it at least once when I visit.'

I sip at my drink, my eyes devouring the whole spectacle, my body alive with his proximity. I'd love to spend more time here—taking in the sights, being a tourist... There's a vibe that I just love. I want to 'do' Chinatown, explore the famous Botanic Gardens, enjoy a Singapore Sling at Raffles Hotel, relax...*with him*.

'I'd love to do the tourist thing.'

I feel his eyes on me. 'Next time we come we'll do just that.'

Next time we come...

I turn to him. Those words are there again but they catch in my throat. I wet my lips. 'Is that a promise, Lucas?'

He curves his hand around the back of my neck, stirring every excited nerve-ending.

'Yes.'

And then he kisses me and the world falls away.

Next time... There's going to be a next time... Oh, yes.

I've always loved this pad. The view, the location, the buzz. But lying here with Eva curled into my side, with the view outstretched before us, it truly is heaven on earth. As good as any paradise island or secluded hideaway.

'I wish we didn't have to leave in the morning.'

She toys with the buttons on my shirt as she says it, her contented sigh warming me through.

I trace circles over her bare shoulder and press a kiss to her head. 'Me too.'

'Thank you for all this.'

She looks up at me, her eyes dark in the soft white glow that comes from the decorative lighting cubes that line the terrace.

'What? For putting so much work into convincing you to go into business with me?' I grin. 'It seems a pretty selfish move, if you ask me.'

She digs me in the ribs and rolls on top of me. 'You know full well you didn't need to do all this.'

'Do I?'

'Yes, you could have documented all of it—in fact, if I dug a bit, I bet I'd find article after article about the fabulous Waring Holdings and its equally fabulous owner.'

'*Fabulous*, am I?'

Her smile turns shy and my heart blooms in my chest at her silent answer. She drops a kiss to my lips and folds her arms over my chest, her chin coming to rest upon them as she looks at me.

'Does that mean I have the job?' I ask.

I'm half joking, half serious. But she's all serious now, quiet, her eyes wavering over my face.

'I have people I've yet to see… It doesn't feel right, cancelling on them.'

'But why waste their time if you've decided?'

'Because they still deserve to be listened to and considered.'

'Are you saying that because you mean it or because you're worried about how your family will react?'

She presses herself off me and rolls onto her back, her eyes looking skyward. 'I'm not scared of them.'

She says the words, but there's an edge that I don't like.

I turn on my side and look down into her face. 'No?'

'I just don't want to hurt them or provoke them further.' Her eyes flick to me. 'I want to get this right— make them see what they did was wrong. But I can't push them out entirely. It's not fair on Mum, for starters, and for all they did wrong they're…they're still…'

'They're still your family.'

'Yes.' It's a whisper.

'So what will you tell them when the time comes? Because it will, Eva. You know as well as I do that our companies working together is the right move.'

I don't say the other thing I'm thinking: *We work, her and I...us.*

'The truth.'

'Which bit?' I test the water. 'The work or the personal—*this*?'

'All of it.'

She nods her head emphatically, surprising me with her confidence.

'This deal gets me what I need. It buys them out of my business, and it buys me my total freedom. It's what I've wanted for so long—to be in control of my own destiny, my future, my company.' She pins me with her brilliant gaze. 'As for me and you...they have to see they've wronged you...' Her voice trails away, a frown marring her brow as her eyes narrow. 'Unless...'

Unease spreads like ice in my veins. 'Unless...?'

'Is there more to it?'

She's looking at me earnestly, searchingly.

'I just don't get it. They're good people, Mum and Dad. And Dad knows that Nate has his moments—well enough to suspect that what you told him was the truth—so why side with him?'

Why? I think about it. I think about what I told her. It's the truth—all of it.

Nate hated me for not stepping in, not saving his arse after he'd screwed up—again. I could've done, but

I didn't. Her father just protected his son…and to hell with what was right, fair.

I rest my hand over her stomach, feel her warmth seep into my palm. I lower my eyes to the touch and use it to ward off the mounting chill.

'There's nothing to tell you that changes anything. It happened just as I told you.'

She's quiet as she considers me, and then she shakes her head and looks back to the view. 'I just don't get it… Nate isn't a bad person deep down—he isn't. I wouldn't look out for him if he wasn't.'

'You would. He's your brother.'

Just as your father protected his son—his real son, his blood.

'No, I wouldn't—not if he didn't deserve it. He's unreliable, sure, and he messes up sometimes. He clearly messed up with you. But he loved you, you were inseparable, and now… Now he—'

She breaks off, as if she can't even voice it.

'He hates me?'

She looks at me, her eyes stabbing me with their pain, eyes that look so similar to Nate's in that moment, filled with the same blaze of hurt he wore the last time I saw him.

'Yes.'

I don't really hear her. I'm transported back five years. To that last argument…to his begging.

'You owe us! You wouldn't be anything without our money! You can save us. How can you refuse?'

Their love shouldn't have been conditional. Mine

certainly wasn't. I thought I was loved. By Nate, by his parents. Eva. And look where it got me.

Shit. Don't tar her with the same brush.

I shut it all down and look at the view.

'Sorry,' she says. 'I know it's hard for you…the past. It's hard for me too—but we have to face it head-on if we're to get through this.'

My eyes fall to hers. 'And will we? Face this together when the time comes?'

She hooks her fingers through my hair, drawing me in. 'Yes. *Together.*'

She kisses me and all my doubts dissolve in the heat of her.

I trust her.

I love her.

And when the time is right I will tell her.

But not before she does what she says she will: confronts her family, Nate, and puts me first. Proves to me that *her* love has no conditions. Then I'll know for sure.

So, do you really trust her?

I groan with frustration, with need, as I kiss her hard, punishingly. I want to trust her—that's the point.

I tear my lips from her mouth and let my mouth travel to her throat. I nip her skin. 'I want you.'

It's as much as I can confess—as much as my heart and body will let me confess.

'I want you too.'

She forks her fingers through my hair, tugging me down, arching her body, her nipples already like marbles beneath her top.

I take one into my mouth, tease her through the fabric, drop my fingers to the apex of her thighs…

For now we have this, and I'm going to take it all. Tomorrow we'll return home and face it together. As one.

CHAPTER THIRTEEN

TUESDAY MORNING REALITY HITS—as it has to—only it's softened by the bed I wake up in: *his*.

The smell of fresh coffee greets me as I stroll into the kitchen and I know he's already gone. He warned me he had to be in Edinburgh early, for a meeting, that he would be away for a couple of days, but the fact he's set the coffee machine going in time for my wake-up call brings the goofiest of smiles to my face.

I could get used to this.

I know I have a huge ordeal ahead, breaking the news of us to my family, but it's the right thing. *We* are right. And the past has to be dealt with. Sooner rather than later. I want this Christmas to be special, I want Lucas in it.

I turn on the radio as I potter around the kitchen. Slade's 'Merry Xmas Everybody' fills the air and I'm dancing. Happy. Truly festive.

I am so convinced everything will be okay that I spend the next few days in a bubble.

By day I work, ticking off my back-to-back meetings as promised, sticking to my plan and being fair to all concerned.

By night I enjoy the countdown to Christmas. I hit the shops, I wrap presents, I decorate my mini-tree, bringing a much-needed pop of colour to the otherwise bland apartment, and I look forward to Friday. To seeing Lucas. My future. Our future.

I don't forget about Friday night's meal. I don't forget that Dad has promised to talk with Nate. I just have faith in my family to get things right this time.

It's Friday. Three days and three nights since I left her warm body in my bed. It feels like an eternity.

I've wanted to ring her—of course I have—but I also wanted to respect her decision to stick to her review process and the meetings she'd lined up.

I didn't want to mess with that.

I didn't want to appear desperate either.

I rake my fingers through my hair and take the stairs to her office, needing to burn off this incessant thrum of energy. I could put it down to excitement at seeing her again, but I know it's also nerves.

I hoped she'd call me, or at least email. But nothing.

And if I'm honest I'm scared she's changed her mind. About us, the business…all of it.

But it's time for our allotted meeting and she hasn't cancelled to avoid it, to avoid me. That has to count for something.

I get to her floor and her PA spies me before I'm across the room, her smile welcoming.

'Ah, Mr Waring, it's lovely to see you again.' She

steps out from behind her desk and offers her hand.
'Can I get you a coffee?'

I don't care what she gets me so long as I see Eva
soon. I shake her hand with a nod. 'Thank you.'

She turns and leads the way to Eva's office; a gentle
rap and she pokes her head through.

'Mr Waring is here.'

I can't make out Eva's response and I strain for it.
Eager to hear her voice.

'You can go on through.'

She opens the door wider and I lose all sight of her
as I seek out Eva.

'Lucas.'

She smiles and pushes up out of her seat to walk towards me, I meet her halfway and hear the door click
shut as her PA leaves us.

She's a vision in pink again. This time a sleeveless
dress that hugs her frame to the knee. Her hair is in a
loose knot at her nape and silver snowflakes dangle
from her ears. I itch to reach for one, to reach for *her*, to
embrace her, to kiss her. A thousand wants and I can't
even speak as I try to keep them contained.

She pinches the corner of her bottom lip with her
teeth, hesitant, but her eyes are alive. 'Are you okay?'

'I'm just absorbing my first sight of you in three days.'

She laughs softly. 'Well, in that case, absorb away.'

She gives a little twirl and I'm undone. My hand
reaches to cup her waist and pull her into me, my lips
find hers.

She feels so good, sounds so good as her startled little whimper ripples through her throat and her hands grip me hard, needy. Her mouth, her tongue—every bit the same. It's intense and wild, and I realise with startling clarity that I could make love to her now, so easily, and her PA is returning with coffee.

Dammit.

I set her away from me, dragging air into my lungs. 'Your PA is bringing me coffee.'

Her fingers tremble as she touches her lips, her confused frown *so* fucking adorable.

'Coffee?'

'I may have agreed to have some.'

Her lips curve upwards, her eyes dance. 'So you're saving her from a scene?'

'Something like that.'

Heat streaks my cheeks and I'm not sure whether it's an alien sheepishness that does it or the lust still raging inside me, but the rap at the door is well-timed.

She smooths her dress out—it already looks perfect—and calls, 'Come in.'

'Here we go—two coffees and some festive treats.' Her PA places a tray on the desk and turns to leave. 'You know where I am if you need anything else.'

Her smile encompasses us both before she leaves, and I get the sneaking suspicion she knows exactly what was going down seconds before.

'She's a smart one.'

'If you mean she's got us pegged, then I'd say you're right.'

She returns to her desk and lifts a mug, places it on a mat before the visitor's chair, a mince pie following suit.

'Why don't we get business out of the way before we...er...?'

'Get carried away again?'

I'm grinning at her, high on her response to me, on what it means for us and the future. Everything is within reach. Everything that matters at least. Her suggestive smile across the desk tells me so.

I feel like I'm rushing to the end of our talk just to get back to where we were when Lucas first arrived.

I've told him I want to work with him. I've told him I've rejected the other offers. I've also made sure he understands it wasn't a simple choice to make—that he did have tough competition despite his claims and his report. Rosalie at Janus Industries, in the main. I liked her, and her offer was almost comparable—*almost*.

And there had been a moment's hesitation when I'd acknowledged to myself that going into business with her would be simpler...that the complication of loving and working with Lucas did go against him. But ultimately I fell in love with the way his business operates too.

'So we're agreed?' he says.

'I think so.'

I rise out of my seat and he follows suit, his eyes fixed on me. My pulse starts to race and I press my palms into the skirt of my dress, moisten my lips.

'So we're done with work?'

I nod. I want to race to him, but I force my pace to slow, my fingers trailing along the desk-edge as I approach him.

He turns to face me, his gaze flitting between my mouth and my eyes, dark, hungry. I reach out and wrap my fingers through the tail end of his tie, wrap and wrap until I'm almost to the knot, and then I pull him down to me.

Yes. No interruptions...no nothing now. This is all about us.

Our lips meet, soft, savouring, sampling. It's blissfully sweet. A moment's reacquaintance before all hell breaks loose with the sweet invasion of his tongue. My insides soar and his hands turn rough, pulling me against him as my grip over his tie tightens.

'I've missed you,' he says against my lips, his hands raking up and down over me.

'I've missed you too.'

He groans at my words, his fingers hooking under the hem of my dress, his palms on my skin, hot and urgent as he forces my dress up. It's at my hips when he lifts me, swinging me onto the desk, his mouth not once releasing me, his tongue delving deeper, driving me to fever pitch.

I wrap my legs around him, breaking our kiss long enough to take hold of his zipper, to ease it down. He's so hard as I draw him out, and my body contracts on a ripple of lustful heat.

'What the actual fuck?'

We freeze. Our heads turn to the door—

Nate!

His seething form fills the doorway.

Fuck.

I shove Lucas back, leaving him to yank his zipper up as I launch to my feet.

My brother looks as if he's about to commit murder.

'I fucking *knew* it.' He strides forward, slamming the door shut behind him, his fist raised. 'You son of a bitch.'

I watch in horror as he swings for Lucas, and then I throw myself forward.

I see a brief second of panic in my brother's face before his fist collides with my face. And then all I feel is pain—acute, throbbing pain—and my ears ring.

I'm on my knees, shaking my head, trying to focus, to get a handle on what's happening.

I can hear scuffling above me.

'See what you made me do!'

My brother is shouting, shoving Lucas back. I try to tell them to stop but I can't make my mouth work.

'I didn't make you do anything,' Lucas says. 'Now back off so I can check she's okay.'

'You've touched her enough, you sick fuck—taking your revenge out on someone too stupid to see it.'

I know what's going to happen even before Lucas's fist makes perfect contact with my brother's jaw, and inside I die.

This is wrong.

All wrong.

I don't want to believe it's happening.

Nate drops to the floor as Lucas rushes to my side and tries to lift me. *No.* I shake him off. Tears that I hadn't known I was shedding sting my cheeks.

'Don't touch me.'

I can't even look at him. Either of them.

It's a mess. A complete and utter mess.

'Get out,' I say, struggling to my knees. My lip smarts…it feels too big for my face. 'Both of you.'

The command is muffled and my cheeks flame in shame, pain, anger.

'But, Eva…' Lucas says softly, his hands hovering over me, not touching, but still there.

I shake my head again, putting the force that I can't give to my voice into action. I turn away from him. 'Get out.'

'Sis, come on.'

'Out! Out! *Out!*'

I stare at them both, my body rigid, and I almost lose it all over again when neither moves. I can't cope with the concern on Lucas's face, the anger and the swelling already building on Nate's, the throbbing pain radiating through my own. It's a real-life nightmare.

Lucas lets go of a ragged breath. 'Okay.' He looks at Nate, his disgust, his hatred, clear as day, and then he shakes his head and makes for the door.

'And don't fucking come back!' my brother throws at him.

I want to shout, to tell him to shut up, but I'm frozen in their hate.

Lucas looks to me for something—anything—but I'm trance-like.

And then he's gone.

'Good riddance,' Nate mutters, rubbing at his jaw.

Slowly, I turn, taking him in. Replaying it all. *'Stupid'* was what he called me. *Stupid.* After everything I've done for him these last few years. Everything he did to bring this raining down on us.

'Stupid…?'

My voice trembles over the simple word. White-hot anger laces every syllable.

He looks to me now, his eyes landing on my lip. 'Shit, Eva—I'm so sorry.'

He moves towards me and I raise my hand to stop him. 'Sorry for hitting me or for referring to me as stupid?'

I know that's what made Lucas snap—he was coming to my defence. It should make me happy. Instead I'm terrified. Terrified of the hatred that filled the room, the hatred between the two people I love. My worst fear coming to fruition.

He shakes his head and looks to the floor, appearing more like a teenager than the thirty-one-year-old he's supposed to be.

'I flipped out. I'm sorry. Seeing you, my little sister…' He raises his eyes to me, his shoulders bunching. 'And him…like that. I mean, for fuck's sake, Eva, you were about to let him screw you over your desk. *Him.*'

I'm still and controlled as I say, 'Who I sleep with is none of your business.'

'It is when it's him, and you know it.'

'Bollocks, Nate. *You* were the one who went behind his back and totally stuffed the company—him included.'

He stares at me, wide-eyed.

'Yes, he told me. He didn't want to. He said I should come to you, make you explain.' My smile is bitter, tight. 'Would you have admitted it if I had, though?'

'Eva—'

He breaks off and I wonder if he's going to lie some more. I can't bear it if he does.

'Look… I made a bad decision, okay? I know that, and I've regretted it ever since, but has he told you the whole story?'

My eyes narrow, a sudden chill making my skin prickle. I wrap my arms around my middle and remind myself that I trust Lucas. *I do.*

'What else is there?'

'He could have saved us, Eva—the whole business. He'd been investing for years on the side. How do you think he got so huge so quickly? He'd been stockpiling money…building up his own funds.'

I swallow. 'Stealing from the company?'

Nate snorts. 'As if! Lucas would never sink that low.'

Relief swamps me and my knees weaken. I plant my hands on the desk. The swell of nausea sudden and disorientating. 'Then what?'

'Don't you see? He was already loaded when the company lost it all.'

'When *you* lost it all.'

'Whatever…' he blurts, brushing off my point. 'I pleaded with him to reinvest. To take his private money and pump it in so we could get back on our feet, keep going, keep working together. We were supposed to be a *team*.'

I laugh—I can't help it. 'Don't you see the irony in that?'

His eyes flicker, pained, vulnerable, and I know he does.

'But he was like my *brother*, Eva, and I begged him—fucking *begged* him.' His voice shakes over the confession. 'And do you know what he said?'

His eyes stare at me accusingly. As if he's seeing Lucas, not me.

'No. Fucking *no*. Can you believe it? After all our family had done for him...all the money Dad had ploughed into the business from the start... He'd be nothing without us—*nothing*.'

'But you betrayed him, and then you lied about it to us all. How could he trust you after that?'

He shakes his head at me. 'You don't *get* it! I even offered to hand over enough shares to give him the majority, put him fully in the driving seat—that should have negated his trust issues. But did he care? Did he *fuck*.'

He forks his hands through his hair and starts to pace.

'I didn't know what to do. The look in Dad's eye when I told him...the disappointment... I couldn't stomach it.'

'So you threw Lucas under the bus instead?'

My tone is low, my eyes unforgiving as I watch him flounder. I can see the anger giving way to guilt, remorse, and it's what I'm hoping for.

'It was *our* company, *our* baby, and he gave up on it—we lost it all.'

'*You* lost it all.'

He looks at me, almost desperate. 'Will you drop the whole "you", "we" shit? What does it matter when it was one and the same company?'

'It makes a world of difference, Nate, and you know it.'

My jaw is throbbing like mad, and it hurts to speak, but I can't let this slide. If Lucas and I are to see a way through this I have to make my family acknowledge that they wronged him. And it needs to start with Nate.

'Just admit it.'

'Why? Because you want to get your end away—?'

The door swings open—no knock, no nothing—and in strides my father.

Jesus, could this day get any better?

'Eva, what the hell is—?'

He breaks off, his eyes landing on me—or more specifically on my flaming lip—and his skin pales as the door closes behind him.

'What happened?'

He softens his stride as he walks towards me, his eyes narrowing over the damage.

'Did Lucas—?'

My entire body flares as I back away from him. 'Don't you *dare* accuse Lucas of this.'

'Then who?'

'Why don't you look to your son—the guy who's to blame for this whole goddamn mess?'

He looks from me to Nate for the first time and his cheeks flood red. 'You struck your sister?'

'He was aiming for Lucas,' I rush out. 'I just got in the way.'

'And that?' He points to the swelling on Nate's jaw.

'Lucas—coming to my defence.'

He shakes his head, disbelieving. 'Is this really what we've come to? Fist fights in the office?'

'Don't you dare get high and mighty, Dad,' I say to him. 'You're not innocent in all of this either.'

He frowns with surprise. 'What does *that* mean?'

'All this hatred towards a man who did nothing wrong, Dad—*nothing*. You should've known—you should've seen through Nate's lies and sorted this mess out long ago, before Lucas lost everything.'

'The man is *loaded*, Eva,' Nate scoffs. 'He hardly lost everything.'

'He lost *us*, Nate—*us*. The only real family he's ever known. How the hell can't you *see* that?'

He stares, dumbstruck, then looks from me to Dad, as if our father will say something to ease the sting of my words. But instead he takes a shaky breath and suddenly seems to age before me. I can see my words sinking in, can feel the weight of them in the air.

Nate gives an awkward laugh. 'Oh, come on— the guy is doing fine. He always lands on his feet. Turns out he never needed us—not really. The man's invincible...'

He says the words but there's no power behind them.

'That's not true, son.'

My father's soft-spoken remark stuns me.

'Eva's right.'

'But…come on…look at him. He's loaded—a billionaire. What do we have that he could possibly think he's missing out on?'

I flip. 'Are you for *real*? You should be running after him, begging his forgiveness.'

'Like hell!' he erupts, staring at us both in disbelief. 'He bailed on *me*.'

'You know what?' I say. 'I used to think it was the shock of Lucas going that left you so broken, always coming to me for help, advice, support. Now I realise he'd probably been covering for you for years—and I ended up doing the same.'

'Hey, easy, honey…'

Dad steps forward, wanting to calm me, but I'm on a roll now. Five years of watching over Nate, coming to a head.

'Don't "easy" me. We were the closest thing to family he had and we turned our backs on him.'

'He turned his back on us first.'

It's Nate who speaks, and I want to swing for him, but my legs are like lead, keeping me rooted, and instead I twist on the spot to glare at him.

'It's true, isn't it? It wasn't the first time you'd messed up?'

Nate hunches forward, back in teenage mode, but his downcast eyes are admission enough.

My hands soar to the air as I fling them towards him and look to Dad. 'You *see*?'

'Yes, honey, I see. But this isn't helping. Why don't you just take up Janus Industries' offer and then we'll see what we can do about addressing the past—it's a separate issue.'

'What?'

'Rosalie's offer,' he says, focusing on the work, the business, and making my head spin at the change in focus. 'Your brother called me—told me she'd been in touch to say you'd rejected her offer, that you'd decided on Waring—'

'Yes, *I* decided, Dad! No one else. *Christ*, is that why you're both here? To tell me what to do?'

'Not tell you, just—'

'Get out.'

'Evangeline, take a breath…calm down.'

'Don't speak to me like I'm a child, Dad.'

'I'm—'

'Go.'

'Look, sis…' Nate tries.

'Don't you "sis" me.' I round on him. 'Until you can bring yourself to apologise to Lucas I don't want to speak to you.'

'Come off it—we've a family dinner tonight.'

I laugh over him. 'Tell Mum I can't make it.'

'Eva—?'

Now it's Dad who speaks.

'What? You'd rather I came and explained the fat lip to her?'

They both flinch.

'No, I didn't think so… I could always lie, I suppose.

It seems we're awfully good at that. Did you *really* believe the tale Nate spun, Dad?'

They look at one another, their open shame enough of an answer.

'How could you take away the only real family he ever knew?'

I shake my head. I still can't understand it. I just know I need them gone.

'I'll tell Mum I'm sick.'

'Eva—'

My dad reaches for me but I back away. The last thing I need is a hug right now—not from him. I need Lucas.

My rejection seems to do the trick and together they walk out. My brother is pulling the door closed when he stops.

'What?' I blurt.

'For what it's worth,' he says, looking at his hand on the handle and then back to me, 'I *am* sorry. I know I've done wrong, but I never wanted you caught in the middle like this.'

And then he's gone.

A heavy silence descends and I'm immobilised. Then I start to shiver. Delayed shock, I suppose. I touch my lip and realise I need ice on it before it truly does balloon and I have to avoid both Mum and all meetings well into next year.

I lift my phone and call Clare. She doesn't hesitate at my random request. My guess is that, having seen Nate, she has a fair idea what I want it for. She probably thinks I lamped him.

If only.

I drop into my chair and hug my middle, trying to ease the shakes.

I need to call Lucas, but I need to have this under control first.

I go straight to my apartment. I don't call into the office on the way. I'm in no mood to see anything but the bottom of a whisky bottle.

She kicked me out. *Me.*

Yeah, I totally get that she's upset—but, Christ, she needed to be taken care of, not left alone with that bastard.

I pour a double and take both the bottle and the glass into the living room, dropping onto the sofa and yanking my tie loose. The memory comes of her taking hold of it earlier, the look of passion and joy in her face...

My hand tightens around the glass and I throw back a mouthful, needing its burn.

Seeing her brother like that, hearing him speak about her like he did, the venom in his voice when he spoke to me.

Fuck.

I hunch forward, my elbows on my knees as I stare down into the amber liquid. It's never going to work. So long as they're around her, *we* will never work.

The way she looked between us both, her confusion, her torment... Who does she care about more? It all played out on her face as plain as day. I'm losing her. I can feel it. And my stomach twists, an ice-cold sweat prickling over my skin.

But we have a business arrangement. She told me that much. It's my one hope to keep her.

Hardly.

She can easily work directly with Maylene and the team in Singapore—she'll expect to. No CEO is going to get involved in the day-to-day. She won't need to interact with me. There'll be no contact.

Christ.

I need to think. Fast.

I know she wants the money to buy her family out of her business. She won't be able to do it immediately— she'll need income first.

But if she *had* the money it would be *Bye-bye, Beaumonts...*

Bye-bye, Beaumonts, and Hello, Waring?

I neck the remainder of my glass and toss the idea around.

I'll make it a condition of the contract. She uses my upfront investment to buy them out and bring me in.

She doesn't have to choose anything on a personal level. It's perfect.

Better than any fist to the face, Nate.

CHAPTER FOURTEEN

AT LEAST TWO hours have gone by since Nate and my father left and I'm hiding out in my office, waiting for the last employee to leave before I venture out. It was bad enough seeing Clare's face when she saw the state of me—I couldn't stand the entire floor gossiping. I've never been so thankful for the small en suite bathroom I have adjacent to my office.

And the mini-fridge.

I take out a cold beer and pop it open, wincing as I press it to my lips.

What a day.

Mum has already texted me back, telling me she hopes I feel better soon. Nate has texted me, too, to say he's sorry again—but it's not me he should be telling—and Dad has asked that I go easy on my brother... It's Christmas after all.

Go easy? Like hell. And I'm angry at him too. Angry because he should have seen the truth. He should have sided with Lucas and made Nate take responsibility for his actions.

What? Like you did when the fight broke out?

I squeeze my eyes tight against the memory. I hardly sided with Lucas. In fact I tried to kick them both out. The heat of the moment and divided loyalties made it impossible to think straight. Maybe it was similar for Dad.

But Lucas did no wrong. In either case.

I drop into my chair and take up my mobile. It's time I called him—screw my nerves… I need him, and I need to apologise.

I dial his number and he picks up in two rings.

'Evangeline.'

His voice is gruff, as if he's been drinking, and my heart squeezes in my chest. 'Hi…' I swallow past the wedge forming in my throat. 'I'm sorry I kicked you out.'

His breath shudders down the phone. 'I guess I can't blame you after that showdown.'

'No… Dad arrived after you left.'

'He did?'

'Yeah…' I trail off, working out how to phrase what I want to ask and realise I just need to come out with it. 'Why didn't you tell me Nate asked you to plough your own money into the business?'

'He brought that up, did he?'

'You could have told me.'

'It doesn't really change anything.'

'It does to Nate.'

'You sound like you agree with him.'

'No!' I rush out, hating his defensive tone.

'Look, I couldn't do it. I couldn't trust him not to lose it again. Every time something happened he'd always throw your family's investment at me—tell me

I'd be nowhere without them. He was so quick to lay that on me, so quick to remind me that I'm an outsider, not one of you. Let's face it, I was never going to be free of that guilt trip. I knew I'd always be beholden no matter what happened.'

'You don't need to defend yourself to me, Lucas. I get it.'

And I do—my heart swells for him and all he's been through. All he went through today too—for which I'm partly to blame.

'How's your hand?'

He gives a hoarse laugh. 'I can land a punch just fine. More importantly, how's your face?'

I can hear his concern and it makes me want to cry. Tears burn the back of my throat. I wish he was here with me. I should've driven to his place rather than hidden like this.

'Eva?'

'It's fine—or it will be soon enough.'

'You shouldn't have got involved. When you went down like that—'

He breaks off, his breath shuddering once more.

'Well, next time I promise to stay well clear—you're on your own.'

I'm trying to make light of it, lift the mood, but he's quiet. His silence is unsettling, and I can feel his hatred towards Nate all the way down the line.

'Look, he wasn't seeing straight,' I say. 'Catching us like that had him completely knocked for six.'

'You're making excuses for him again?'

'In this case it's justified. But as far as business goes, and the past, he's on his own—no more cleaning up after him.'

'Good.'

The line goes quiet again. The question burning to get out: *Does he still want there to be an 'us'?* But I'm scared. It doesn't matter that he has hinted strongly at a future—that was before the showdown with my brother, before I fell apart in front of them both.

'Lucas?' I say.

'Eva?' he says at the same time.

Hope sparks within me. 'You go first.'

'I want to amend our agreement.'

His words are clear as day, businesslike, and I struggle to shift gear, from personal to professional.

'What do you mean?'

'You want your family out of your company, yes?'

'You know I do.'

'Well, that works for me too, clearly.'

'My intention is to buy them out as soon as my sales revenue is big enough. It shouldn't take—'

'I want to give you the money now. So you can do it upfront.'

I shake my head. 'Look if you're worried about them interfering, they wouldn't dare.'

'What? Like your brother just didn't dare?'

Before I can speak he carries on.

'I'm not taking any chances.'

I hesitate. 'Okay…'

'But I want something in return.'

So many things stream through my mind, and hope is rising with every one.

I want us. I want you. I want you to tell your family we're together, that there's no getting between us.

'What is it that you want?'

'I want in.'

I frown, a cold tremor running down my spine as I straighten. 'You want *in*?'

'The twenty-five per cent share they currently have—I want it. We can come up with a gradual repayment of the shares over time—say a couple of years, which I imagine isn't too dissimilar to your current plan—but...'

'Back up, Lucas.' I struggle to draw breath, disappointment making my lungs contract. I can't believe what he's saying. What he's focusing on. 'Are you telling me you want me to replace my family with *you*?'

'If you want to look at it that way, then, yes. I don't want them anywhere near our arrangement going forward.'

It's all about revenge.

That's what they said and I didn't believe it. But then why was he so determined to push them out? Why insist on their share? Unless there's some truth to it?

And what about all I had told him about making it my own? Being beholden to no one. Did he not care about any of that? Him of all people...

'You told me this wasn't about revenge...you told me this was about wanting my product.'

'And it *is*, Eva.'

'Then why ask for a share? Why make me choose between my family and you?'

'Don't you see? I'm trying to avoid exactly that. There's no need for personal attachment on the surface. Your family can't resent you for making a sound business decision, and what goes on behind closed doors is our business.'

This just gets worse. Does he really want to dismiss us as some kind of fling? A dirty little secret?

'Oh, my God, Lucas—you *really* think that's the solution?'

'I don't know, Eva. I just know I can't face seeing you hurt like you were today.'

'There are other ways.'

'Name one?'

Being honest and open about our relationship, our love.

But what if it isn't love for him? What if after all he has said he doesn't feel the same way?

I can't bring myself to ask. I can't be that eighteen-year-old, wearing her heart on her sleeve again only to have it thrown back in her face.

Instead I ask a question just as revealing. 'So tell me, Lucas, if I say no are you taking your offer off the table?'

Silence.

'Lucas?'

'Yes, Eva.' He sounds resigned. 'If you don't let me buy in, the offer is off the table.'

My ears ring, disbelief coursing wildly through my

blood. I feel trapped, backed into a corner by the man I love with all my heart.

Scrap not wanting to be my eighteen-year-old self. I *am* her. Humiliated and rejected in one fell swoop. Even worse, I feel manipulated, controlled—*by him*.

I look at the family photo that sits on my desk, the similarities between him and them as unbelievable as they are unbearable. And I laugh, the sound high-pitched and alien.

Well, no more. I won't be controlled or manipulated by either of them. Yes, Rosalie might have been referred by Nate and my father, but she can give me what I need.

Without this.

Without the heartache.

My chest pangs painfully and I grip the phone tighter. 'In that case you can shove your offer, Lucas.'

'Eva, don't be ridiculous.'

I can hear his shock and it gives me the strength I need to hold my ground. There'll be time for tears later.

'There's no need to fly off the handle,' he says.

'If you really believe that then you haven't listened to a word I've said over the past couple of weeks.'

'Seriously, Eva, don't do this. Take the offer…at least think about it.'

'I don't need to think about anything, Lucas. It's over. All of it. *Over.*'

I cut the line dead, my entire being thrumming.

I'm alone. Truly alone.

And now I let the tears fall.

Ten years and I'm still no wiser.

I only have myself to blame.

Give over, Eva, you are wiser!

The old me would have rolled over and taken what Lucas offered. I can at least be proud that I took control—of both him and my family. I held my ground and my product will have a home with Rosalie.

So why do I feel as if I've lost everything?

I stare at the phone as if it's magically going to start ringing again, and when it doesn't I don't know what to do.

I want to ring her back. Hell, I want to drive straight over and make her see sense.

Working together gives us a way through this. A way that doesn't make it personal.

But it is personal. You love her. You let Nate come between you ten years ago and now you've let him do the same again. You fool.

I toss the phone aside and reach for the bottle.

One more.

One more to numb this.

One more to make me think clearly.

I watch the liquid slosh into the glass and know I don't need to think any more clearly.

Because I love her, I can't take her from her family. For all I said I'd make her choose, when it came to it in that room I realised I couldn't.

My gut turns over. I lost her before, but back then I'd never really had her.

Now I have...

CHAPTER FIFTEEN

I'M OUT IN the garden, avoiding them, and they know it. But, hell, it's Christmas Day, my favourite day of the year. I'm supposed to be happy and instead sadness hangs around me like an aura.

I only have to walk into a room and everyone else catches it. Even my mother's usual festive beam is dialled down.

Granted, the fact that Nate and I still aren't speaking doesn't help. But Mum knows the true extent of my sadness. She guessed it for the most part—my age-old feelings for Lucas were obvious to her astute gaze, and the second she probed it all came rushing out, a week of keeping it to myself proving too much.

And I think she's told Dad. I can see it in the way he looks at me. But he hasn't said a word to acknowledge it. It's driving me crazy, but I don't feel strong enough to have it out with him. I feel broken. Torn in two. And to what end?

It's not as if Lucas loved me back.

There's a whimper at my feet and I look down to see

my parents' Golden Lab, Frodo, staring up at me, his ears back.

'I know, kiddo. Sucks, doesn't it?'

I tickle his head and look out across the lawn. It's pretty out here. It's nearly lunchtime and the frost hasn't lifted so everywhere is crisp and white. Almost as festive as snow itself.

I breathe in fresh air and let it seep out in a puff of white. I'll have to go back in soon. I can't avoid them for ever.

'Eva?'

I turn. Mum's hanging out of the kitchen doorway.

'Could you give me a hand with the potatoes, love?'

I give a soft sigh and whisper, 'Time's up, Frodo.' Then I call back, 'Sure!' and start towards her, Frodo trotting in step beside me.

The festive favourite 'White Christmas' leaks through the gap she leaves in the door and my heart squeezes.

You've only yourself to blame, giving your heart away a second time.

'I thought Nate was on potato duty?' I say as I enter the kitchen and strip off my coat.

She's pulling the turkey out of the oven. Its scent fills the room, warm and inviting. But still my insides fail to smile.

'I've sent him to talk with your father.'

'Talk?' I pull open the larder door and root around for the potatoes. 'Sounds ominous.'

'They need their heads knocking together. I've simply led the way.'

'*Mum*, what have you said?'

'Only what needed saying.'

'Which is…?'

'Never mind that—you just focus on those potatoes and leave their foolishness to me.'

She's basting the turkey, her manner brooking no argument. Not that I have the energy for one.

'And smile, please, Eva. It's Christmas and I have faith that all will be well again soon.'

I lug the heavy sack of spuds on to the side and swing the larder door shut, wishing I had her confidence. But then she isn't the one with the broken heart.

'Right, how many do you need?'

Mum goes about giving instructions and I do as she asks, my smile forced and firmly planted. I even start to sing with her. Nothing like a good Christmas tune to get you in the mood.

Not that I am—not at all.

But I'm trying. I really am.

'I think you've peeled more than enough, love.'

'Huh?' I look at her and see her frown, full of concern. I look back to the peeled potatoes, far in excess of the twenty she requested. *Oh, dear.*

'You always tell me it's better to have too many than too few,' I force out jovially. 'And there's always bubble and squeak tomorrow, right?'

'True.' She gives me a smile that I know says *It'll be okay* and goes back to her turkey.

I go back to peeling the spuds. And then stop. *No more potatoes*.

If only I could stop loving Lucas as easy.

But if ten years without him didn't work, why will the future be any different?

Dusk is settling as I pull up outside the house I once called home. It's set back from the road, its private drive bordered by trees and old-fashioned lamps, their soft glow lighting up the well-maintained garden. Well-maintained and just the same as it was the last time I was here…

Five years ago.

The night I realised I was no longer welcome.

And yet you're here now.

I drop my eyes to the steering wheel, to my knuckles that are white as I grip it tight. Maybe this isn't a good idea. It's Christmas. A day for families. A day for the Beaumonts. Not me, the outsider.

My eyes drift to the house, to the bedroom window top right—Eva's room. As if by magic her light comes on. I can vaguely make out someone moving around and then the curtains are drawn and a silhouette remains— *Eva?*

I'm no longer thinking. I'm getting out of the car and walking up the drive, my eyes fixed on that shadow, my body following my heart.

It's time I gave her the choice.

Time I wore my heart on my sleeve and took a chance.

I can feel no worse than I do already. Because I am nothing without her. Life has no meaning without her in it.

I need her to know that. I need her to know it's not her product, it's not her family, it's *her* that I want, that I love.

What the Beaumonts do with that is up to them.

I only care what Eva does.

I sit next to Nate, and Mum and Dad sit across from us. The table is fit to burst, with elaborate candelabra stuffed with holly, baubles, berries and pinecones— I spent several distracted hours making them—and a feast that could feed the entire village.

But no one is eating. No one is speaking.

If not for Frodo's intermittent whine for food and the gentle hum of Christmas carols playing it would be as quiet as a morgue.

I look to Mum, to the concern bright in her eyes, and guilt swamps me. I try for a smile. 'This looks lovely. Thanks, Mum.'

She doesn't seem to hear me. Instead she looks to Nate, and then to my father.

'Right, you two—out with it. I'm not having Eva force herself to get through dinner without hearing from you first.'

Dad looks at Nate, and I sense my brother shift in his seat.

'I've said I'm sorry…to her…to Dad…'

'And…?' Mum presses.

'And I *will* apologise to Lucas too. I *am* sorry for what I did. I just assumed he'd be okay. I mean…he's Lucas. He was always okay.'

He shrugs awkwardly, his smile filled with remorse as he looks to me for forgiveness.

'I need you to understand that, sis. I was hurt when he wouldn't help me, and I lashed out. I lied, and I'm sorry… I guess I was always a little envious of how good he was at everything, and too selfish to care about the consequences.'

I hear what he's saying, and I can read that he means it too, and my heart lifts a little. But it doesn't change how things have worked out. It doesn't change how Lucas feels for me.

'And you, David?' My mother turns to my father. 'What do *you* have to say?'

He clears his throat. 'I'll go with Nate. I'll make sure Lucas realises that we were in the wrong, and that you shouldn't be tainted by this, Eva. If you want to work with him—'

Mum elbows him none too subtly in the ribs and he clears his throat again.

'If you want to *be* with him, then you have our blessing.'

I want to cry and laugh at once. So much, too late. 'Thanks, Dad, I appreciate it.'

'Good.'

'But you don't need to worry. I've decided to sign with Rosalie.'

My father's frown is immediate, as is my brother's.

'Why?'

My throat clogs as my vision blurs, and I try to swallow, to force it back. I can't bring myself to say that it's over between Lucas and I. All of it—over.

'Sis…?'

Nate's voice is soft, his hand on my shoulder aimed to soothe, and I shake my head. My fingers tremble as I press them to my lips.

'He's gone… He's gone and he's not coming back.'

'But—'

My father's voice is drowned out by the ancient doorbell chiming through the house and Frodo's bark. Everyone looks in the direction of the hall, momentarily frozen, and it's my mother who comes alive first, standing and brushing off her skirt.

'How's that for timing?'

She bustles out, Frodo on her tail, but she's hardly gone a second before her voice reaches us.

'Eva, darling, you have a visitor.'

A visitor? On Christmas Day?

There's only one person I'd dare hope would turn up.

'Don't keep him waiting,' my father urges.

I rise up and head out into the hallway on autopilot. Mum is at the front door. Frodo is on his hind legs, fussing over my visitor.

Over—*Lucas.*

My heart leaps inside my chest, and my footing falters just as his eyes meet mine.

'Ah, there she is,' says Mum, turning to face me, her smile one of beaming encouragement as she leaves

Lucas and walks towards me. 'Come on, Frodo, let's get you some turkey.'

She gives my arm a gentle squeeze as she passes, but I'm barely aware of the contact as I drown in his gaze, forcing my legs to close the distance between us.

'What are you doing here?' I manage to say.

'Isn't it obvious, Evangeline?'

The sound of my name from his lips runs through me, comforting as honey. Is he really here? Is this some sick joke? Some weird dream that I'm going to wake up from any second?

'The last time we spoke you wanted my product with a bit of fun on the side.'

He cringes, his fists flexing at his sides. 'I couldn't care less about the product.'

I scoff—I can't help it—but it dies at the sincere look in his eyes. They're swimming. Or is it only mine that are? Making it impossible to focus clearly?

'Sorry—of course I *care* about your product, and Janus Industries will do an amazing job, I'm sure, but what I mean is... What I'm here for is... Hell, I love you, Evangeline.'

He reaches for me, his hands cupping my arms, his touch as real and as warming as his words.

He loves me...he truly loves me.

My head spins as I blink through the tears and see the passion, the love, in his warm brown gaze.

'I've loved you for far too many years to count,' he says softly. 'I wish I'd just come out and told you, but I was scared. Scared to take that leap...scared of putting you in the middle, making you choose and having you regret it.'

I shake my head. 'I'd never regret *you*.'

He groans and pulls me against him, his hug so tight I'm winded, and then his hands are in my hair, he's tilting my head up to meet him, and his lips are on mine, crushingly sweet.

I kiss him back, but it's not enough. I am finally free to say the words that have been burning through me for so long. No more fear. No more doubt.

I pull away, my hands framing his face as I look up into his eyes. 'I love you too.'

His grin is long and slow, and his eyes are moving over my face as though he's reading my sincerity, and then he breaks away, his voice soft as he says, 'I'm so glad you said that because...' He rummages in his pocket. 'I have something for you.'

'You bought me a present? But I haven't—'

I look down as he raises his hand. On his palm rests a small red box.

A small red ring box.

My lips part on a rush and my eyes lift to his, wide and questioning. 'Lucas...?'

'You're all the family I could ever want—you, me... kids if we so desire. I don't know how we navigate this with your family, but I know this is the right place to start. By giving you the choice.'

I watch as he drops to one knee on the weathered coir mat, his eyes not once leaving mine. I press my fingers to my lips, keeping back the sob that threatens. I don't want to break this moment.

He opens the box and inside is the most beautiful pink diamond ring—*pink*.

'Is it—?' I break off. It can't be. And yet I know that it is. This is Lucas.

'It's an Argyle Pink Diamond. It seemed very…you.'

My laugh is soft and shaky. 'It's exquisite.'

'So are you.' He blinks up at me once, twice. 'Will you marry me, Evangeline Beaumont?'

I am trembling. My head is shaking. My eighteen-year-old self is dancing like crazy inside.

'No?' He frowns, panic creasing his forehead, his hand dropping just a little. 'I'll work hard to make amends with your father…your brother. I'll do everything I can—'

'Shh…' I drop my hand to his lips, silencing him, laughter bubbling through the tears. 'Yes, I'll marry you—*yes!* Now, hurry and put that ring where it belongs and maybe I'll believe this is real.'

'Oh, it's real, all right.'

His grin is so wide, so happy, as he does as he's told, sliding the ring in place.

'If it doesn't fit I can—'

'It's perfect!'

I give my finger a little wiggle, watching the diamond catch the light in the porch, and then I start to sob and laugh all at once. I drop to my knees, flinging my hands around his neck, and kiss him hard, every ounce of excitement, happiness and love poured into it.

He breaks away first. His skin is delightfully flushed, his eyes bright.

'Merry Christmas, wife-to-be.'

Evangeline. Wife-to-be. The words work the same magic and my heart flutters and swells with sheer joy.

'Merry Christmas, Lucas.'

EPILOGUE

Christmas Day, one year later

'MUM, WILL YOU stop flapping? Dinner is going to be great.'

'But she's a chef—a celebrity chef—what if it's awful?'

I laugh. I can't help it. Ever since Nate brought home his new girlfriend, Florence, six months ago, Mum has gone into panic mode, not wanting to scare the woman off.

Not that I blame her. Florence has been great for Nate. He'd come a long way since he and Lucas cleared the air, and then he met Florence and the transformation was complete.

Mum looks at me as if she's going to tape my mouth shut. 'Really? You think laughter is going to help right now?'

I take pity and give her a quick squeeze. 'Mum, how many Christmas dinners have you cooked?'

'Too many to count.'

'And how many have gone wrong?'

She frowns. 'Too many to count.'

Okay, bad choice.

'Sorry to disturb the private party.'

Lucas appears in the kitchen doorway—my incredibly handsome saviour.

'But your dad's breaking out the champagne and itching to do a toast.'

He looks at me pointedly and a small smile lifts my lips as we share a silent exchange.

'Come on, Mum. Champagne will make everything better.'

We coax her into the living room just as Dad pops the cork and begins to pour.

I take in the entire scene. Everyone is happy, content—even Frodo is asleep in front of the fire—and I know it's about to get better. Inside my heart swells and Lucas wraps his arm around me as Dad starts to fill the last flute.

'Just a small one for me, Dad.'

He stops pouring and they all look at me, concern flaring. My smile grows. I look up at Lucas, search his deep brown gaze and share my elation with him.

'We have some news.'

The room falls silent. Everyone is waiting and I let Lucas finish it for me.

'We're pregnant.'

Mum gives a dizzying squeal. The men chortle. Congratulations stream through the air as Dad hands out the glasses and gives me my mini-one with a kiss to the cheek.

Nate comes up to us, patting Lucas on the back before giving me a hug. 'I'm so happy for you both.'

'Thank you.'

I look up at Lucas. He knows what I'm going to say next and part of me wants that final nudge from him first. I get it in the form of a kiss to the forehead and a squeeze around the waist.

'That's not all,' I say, my eyes returning to Nate. 'I'm going to need someone to look after things while I'm out of action, and I can't think of anyone I'd rather have than you—if Dad can spare you, that is?'

Nate colours. His eyes blaze. 'For real, sis?'

He knows how much this means. It's the biggest statement I—*we*—could make to show that the past is long since buried.

'For real.'

'You've got it.'

He pulls Florence into his side and offers his glass to the room. 'To the Beaumonts, the Warings and the mini-Beaumont-Warings!'

Laughter fills the room and my tummy gives the smallest flutter, calling my hand to it. Lucas traces the move, his hand coming to rest over mine.

'To family,' I say, raising my glass.

And we all drink to that.

* * * * *